"Kelton tr[...] [...]f the immortals
of literatur[...]

— [...] Herald-Post

"The mo[...] [...]nn."

— [...]dy in the West

"Western storyteller Kelton returns for his fortieth-plus
novel, a sequel to 1978's The Good Old Boys that again features hang-loose Hewey Calloway, circa 1910, as his lov-
able old 'Smiling Country' of West Texas fades into the
automobile age.... Old-timey dialogue, newly minted,
rhetorical stretchers, and whopping good humor right out
of Twain."

—Kirkus Reviews on The Smiling Country

"The fast-moving Cloudy in the West succeeds as a young
adult novel, traditional Western, and an all-around good
read."

—Fort Worth Star-Telegram

"Elmer Kelton has won six Spur Awards—considered
the Oscar for Western writers—for his novels. He should
probably start making room on his mantel for number
seven.... One of Kelton's best works.... Kelton's novel
is short on violence and long on character, accurately
depicting the time, people, and places of post–Civil War
Texas.... As usual Kelton peppers his novel with authentic dialogue, humor, and salty characters.... The
Pumpkin Rollers is Kelton at his best. And as his awards
attest, his best is really good."

—The Herald (Rock Hill, South Carolina)

Other books by Elmer Kelton

MASSACRE
AT GOLIAD

Elmer Kelton

A TOM DOHERTY ASSOCIATES BOOK
NEW YORK

MASSACRE AT GOLIAD

A Forge Book
Published by Tom Doherty Associates, LLC
175 Fifth Avenue
New York, NY 10010

Forge® is a registered trademark of Tom Doherty Associates, LLC.

ISBN: 0-812-57489-3

First Forge edition: September 1999

Printed in the United States of America

0 9 8 7 6 5 4 3 2 1

Author's Note

In the Texas revolution against Mexico, Mexican troops won all the important battles except two: the first one and the last. Between those, the Texians (the early settlers prior to statehood) lost one after another to the numerically superior forces of General Antonio López de Santa Anna.

Everyone knows about the Alamo. Fewer, outside of Texas, know about the massacre at Goliad, where more than twice as many Texians died. The difference was that in the Alamo they fought to the death. At Goliad they were made prisoners, led out and murdered.

A root cause of the revolution—but by no means the only one—was a vast racial and cultural difference between the native Mexican people and the Americans who had come to settle among them in various colonizations since about 1823. Mexico encouraged these settlers at first, seeing them as a potential buffer against the Comanches and other hostile Indians. Men of good will worked hard for understanding between Americans and Mexicans, none more diligently than Stephen F. Austin, the Father of Texas.

But even the gentle and trusting Austin finally had to concede that President Santa Anna was a vain and hopeless tyrant. Like many others before and since, he began as a liberator but grasped for power until he became a ruthless dictator, capriciously holding life and death in his hands. Not only the Texas Americans but many Texas Mexicans and citizens of northern Mexican states rebelled against him. Most of the true old Texian settlers continued to regard themselves as loyal citizens of Mexico, in revolt against Santa Anna, not against the country. Indeed, the defenders of the Alamo—Mexican as well as American—fought and died beneath the Mexican flag of 1824.

Texians under spirited old Ben Milam drove federal troops out of San Antonio in the fall of 1835 and dogged them to the Rio Grande. In response, Santa Anna butchered his way across northern Mexico, putting insurgents to the sword wherever he found them, then crossed into Texas.

The determined resistance at the Alamo surprised and slowed him, giving Sam Houston time to strengthen his defensive force. At Goliad, indecisive commander James W. Fannin delayed an ordered retreat until too late and was surrounded by Mexican troops under General José Urrea. After a costly battle, Fannin surrendered his command on Urrea's good-faith pledge of fair treatment. The dictator countermanded that promise. On Palm Sunday some three hundred and forty prisoners were marched out of the old mission in groups and shot.

Because the firing squads were smaller than the numbers of victims assigned to them, some men were able to break and run between volleys. A few more than twenty are known to have escaped. Some joined Sam Houston in time for his crushing defeat of Santa Anna at San Jacinto.

By then the overconfident self-styled Napoleon of the West had divided his forces and force-marched ahead of the larger body in the hope of catching Houston's little army before it could escape into Louisiana. Santa Anna was contemptuous of his own men, declaring that it was their great privilege to be allowed to die for his honor. He disregarded the suffering they endured by being ill-clothed and poorly equipped for Texas' cold, wet winter. His troops had already been decimated by sickness before Houston's embittered men suddenly turned with a vengeance and drove them reeling into the mud of Buffalo Bayou, where the carnage wrought upon them was horrendous.

In an attempt to escape, Santa Anna donned the

nondescript uniform of a common soldier but was captured and brought trembling before the wounded Sam
Houston. Most of the Texians wanted to hang him then
and there, but Houston counseled peace. Dead, Santa
Anna could sign no treaties. Alive, he could—and did—
acknowledge that Texas was free.

Chapter One

In his later years Joshua Buckalew seldom spoke of Goliad and the terrible thing which happened there. Even in his old age there were nights when the memory returned in a dream and he would wake up suddenly with the cold sweat breaking, the horror as vivid as it had been in his youth.

Yet there was fierce pride in the memory too, for Joshua Buckalew ever afterward considered himself one of the original Texans. He had been a witness to the birth of Texas at Bexar and Goliad and on the marsh-bound prairie of San Jacinto. So, as each of his sons came of age to understand—and later his grandsons—he would tell them the story that they might share his pride in their heritage, and that they might realize and value the awful sacrifice other men had made for Texas.

Always, he began the story long before Goliad. He began it where it had begun for him, one early-spring day in Tennessee. . . .

*   *   *

I could have whipped the Keefer brothers without even breaking a sweat, provided I took them one at a time. But the two together were a mite of excess. They had me staggering in the dust of the crossroads where Gailey's Grocery dispensed everything from harness leather and red calico to raw corn spirits in a jug. Dogs barked. Men and boys cheered and whooped and stood back to give us room. Entertainment was scarce in those parts—a horserace occasionally, a shooting match, a barn-raising or a dance. A good fist fight was usually certain to stir the betting blood. But nobody was betting this time. They could tell that I was fixing to get my plow cleaned good and proper.

I was twenty-one then, five feet eleven and tough as mule-hide. But that wasn't enough. I kept lashing out with my fists at Smiley Keefer and trying with my elbows to knock loose from Snag Keefer's heavy weight on my back. Snag clung like a burr under a pantsleg.

I puffed, the breath coming hard. "This ain't noways a fair fight . . . I didn't go . . . to fight the both of you."

"You got us anyhow." Snag tried to sink his teeth into my ear.

I shifted my weight and threw Snag off balance, sliding him onto his back in the dust. I landed with both knees in Snag's belly. I turned to see where Smiley was and caught a faceful of his fist. These were plowmen, the Keefers, and a plowman's fists are as hard as a hickory knot.

I saw my brother Thomas edge through the crowd.

"Thomas!" I yelled. "Come and help me!"

Thomas was tall and strong, and he had a face that could be as grim as a hangman. He was grim now. He sat himself down in an open spot on the porch and eased the butt of his Kentucky longrifle to the ground.

I never was one to beg for help. Both Keefers were rushing me again. Their weight brought me down and crushed the breath from me. All I had left was a bruised and angry spirit.

"Now, Josh," gritted Smiley, "let's hear you holler quit."

They twisted my arms. The shame of defeat was as bad as the pain. I threshed and pitched. Cloudiness came over my eyes. I heard a firm voice say, "Give up, Josh. You're makin' a fool of yourself." Thomas hovered over me.

I clamped my teeth together tightly to keep from hollering out. Smiley Keefer put more pressure on my arm.

Thomas Buckalew said, "All right, boys, the fun's over. Let him up."

The Keefers waited too long. Thomas grabbed a fistful of hair in each hand, then cracked their heads together. "I said it's over now!"

The Keefers let go and jumped back the way men will jump away from an angry bull that might come up fighting. I arose, eyes blazing, but my knees betrayed me. I knelt, unable to stay up.

Thomas said flatly, "Git your rifle and let's be a-movin'. Pa wants to talk to us."

It was a minute before I had enough breath to speak. "What for?"

"That colonel what's-his-name from Texas has been by the place again. Pa's got that glow in his eyes."

Thomas let me struggle to my feet without help. He stood back, making it plain that he disapproved of my foolishness. The crowd was scattering. I swung around to glare at the Keefers, who leaned against the porch, still breathing hard. Snag was tipping a jug over his arm.

Thomas caught my sleeve and said roughly. "The mail has done left. You lost the fight; now let it go."

"You didn't even ask me how come I was fightin' them."

"I don't reckon as how I care. A man ought to have more pride than to git hisself stomped with half the settlement watchin', and laughin' at him."

"They were pickin' on poor old Muley Dodd."

"*Everybody* picks on Muley Dodd. Besides, I didn't see him."

"He was scared. Minute I hit Snag, Muley lit out arunnin'."

"Josh, you can't spend your life pickin' up after Muley. The Lord chose to short Muley on brains, and it's too bad. But it ain't up to you to be his everlastin' keeper."

"Somebody's got to help him. He can't help hisself."

I limped at first as we walked down the dusty wagon road, each of us carrying a Kentucky rifle. The late-afternoon sun slanted into our faces, for the Buckalew home lay west of the settlement. That was the way it had always been with the Buckalews: always west of the settlement.

Muley Dodd waited for us down the road, his hat in his hand, his eyes afraid. Short, stooped a little, Muley had the first whisker of manhood soft on his face. Ragged hair touched his frayed collar. He started talking when we were still fifty feet away. "Josh, I didn't go to leave you there. I didn't noways mean to run. The Devil got in me, and I was afeared. It was the Devil made me run."

Impatient, Thomas said, "It wasn't the Devil caused you to light out, Muley. It was the Keefers."

I cut a sharp glance at my brother. "Hush, Thomas." I walked up to Muley Dodd and put my hand on his shoulder. "Don't fret now, Muley. It's done over with. They ain't fixin' to bother you again."

"You sure, Josh?" Muley brightened up. "Did you whup 'em good? You're a real friend, Josh. And next time there's a fight, I won't run away. I'll stay right there and help you."

It wasn't so, but I nodded like I believed it. "Sure you will, Muley."

We walked on down the road, us Buckalews, Muley standing and watching us with his hat still in his hand. Thomas said, "Josh, you know he'll always run. He'll be runnin' the last day he lives. You can't protect him forever."

We came to a field where a mule stood waiting in endless patience, tied to a stump. At the turnrow lay my wooden plow. I had hired out to old man Higgins for a spell of work the year before, and Pa had made me take my pay in this plow instead of cash. Pa had declared: "Every man needs a plow of his own, time he comes of age. Money is soon spent. But give you a plow and you got somethin' that'll serve you for years."

It was true, I would have to admit. But I'd always said I'd rather stand back and admire Mother Nature than scratch her face with the point of a plow. A man got almighty tired sometimes of working up and down the rows all day, staring an old mule in the rear.

Thomas said, "Better fetch the mule."

Thomas was only a couple of years older than me, but times he acted as if the difference was ten. With Thomas, day was day and night was night; wrong was wrong and right was right. You drew a line and you stayed on one side of it. You didn't step over it, ever. I wondered sometimes where Thomas had inherited that stiff-backed way. It hadn't come from Pa.

The Buckalew home was of a mixed architecture. It had begun long ago as a log cabin but had been extended and enlarged with rough-sawed lumber through the years, as the lumber became available and the family fortunes had allowed us to buy or barter for it. At one time a lot of Buckalews had lived there. But gradually each came of age to go on his own. The boys went west, and the girls married off. Now there were only Pa and the oldest son, Lott, who was to inherit the place according to family custom. And there were Thomas and me.

Pa sat hunched on the hewn-log steps, puffing his pipe and taking his rest. He still worked hard, Titus Buckalew did. But it seemed like he couldn't take as much of it as he used to. He had worn out too many plows, outlived too many mules. He had cleared this land from virgin timber, by himself at first, then with sons to help him as each came along in his own due time. Lott had a large family of his own now.

Pa's old pipe stood black against the white of his beard as he stared at me. I couldn't see any surprise in the pale blue of his eyes. "Mule drag you, Joshua?"

I never did lie to Pa. "No, sir."

"And you didn't fall out of no tree. So I take it you been fightin'."

"Yes, sir."

"Win?"

"No, sir."

The old man frowned and knocked the pipe against the hard heel of his hand to jar the burned tobacco out. "If you got to fight, at least you ought to win."

"Next time, Pa."

His brow twisted into deep furrows, which came easy to him. "That Colonel Ames, he's been by again, talkin' to me about Texas."

Thomas said, "Pa, ain't it a little late in life for you to be thinkin' about faraway places any more?"

"Not for myself. It's you two that I been frettin' about. It's high time you had a chance to take and do somethin' for yourselves, like your brothers have done."

"You wantin' us to leave, Pa?" I asked.

"No, son, it ain't that I *want* you to. A man don't like sayin' good-bye to his young. But it's the way of life. You can see for yourself, there ain't nothin' left here for a growed man. If you ain't already got your land, you never will get it. What we got here will be just about enough for Lott, once I'm gone. Ever since the first Buckalew come across the big water, they've kept a-lookin' west. I done it, in my day. Your brothers have done it. Now I reckon it's your time."

My skin prickled with excitement. "You think we ought to go to Texas?"

"That's for you to say, not me. But Colonel Ames, he talks like it's a powerful good country for a young man to go and build him a life."

The weariness was suddenly gone from me. "Texas! I been hearin' a right smart about it. The Fancher boy went there last year, him and that Whipple girl he married. And the Smith family. And the year before that, old Henry Leech, only he died along the way."

Thomas nodded. The excitement was touching him too, which was a seldom thing. "The Fanchers got a letter from their boy awhile back. He's right taken with the country, Pa."

Pa drew silently on his pipe, enjoying the tobacco. "The colonel, he says this Stephen F. Austin has got him a colony there, and he'll let a man take up more land than he could accumulate here in a lifetime. All that land, just for the askin'. Of course, you'd have to build her from scratch, but us Buckalews, we always done that."

Thomas frowned. "One thing, Pa, you might not've thought about. Texas ain't in the United States. It's part of Mexico. Us Buckalews have been Americans ever since Grandpa froze his feet that winter with George Washington."

"Governments never did mean no awful lot to us Buckalews, son. We always been so far out front that they never was any bother to us. Anyhow, there's been a-plenty of Americans gone there already. I doubt as you'll see much difference." He was silent awhile, studying first one son, then the other. "Something else: you're both of a marryin' age, and neither one has got you a woman."

Thomas shrugged. I didn't say anything.

Pa said, "Colonel Ames tells me a married man gets twice as much land in Texas as a single man. That's somethin' to consider. I don't expect you're apt to find many unattached females down there. Best play the game safe and take one with you. A bird in the hand, as they say." He looked at me. "How about that Merribelle Keefer, Joshua? She's been chasin' around you like a bear after honey."

I shook my head. "She'd be a burden."

"They all are. But think of that extra land."

"She's not the prettiest I ever saw. And I don't love her."

"Love wears off, and looks change. Main thing is that she can cook. You'd be surprised, too, how she can help keep your bed warm in the wintertime."

"Pa, I've tried her." All of a sudden I felt my face turning red. "Her cookin', I mean. She's not for me."

Humor flickered in Pa's eyes. He turned to Thomas. "How about you?"

"I've never seen a woman I'd marry."

"You always expect too much, Thomas, that's your weakness. You got to learn to bend a little. Women are human. There never was but one perfect man, and I doubt there ever *was* a perfect woman."

Thomas shook his head. "There's still none here I'd want to marry."

Pa shrugged. "Well, that's up to you. Down yonder, you ain't apt to find anything except Mexican girls."

Thomas said flatly, "I know we won't be marryin' one of *them*."

Chapter Two

We started when the warm spring sun brought the green rise of new grass. We said our good-byes and pointed the wagon-tongue southwestward, angling to cut across a corner of Mississippi.

There had been a brief sadness at the time of parting, and there would be sad moments again when the awful finality of those long miles of separation at last came home to me. Thomas's jaw was set square and sober, for he was thinking on these things. But for me, riding ahead on a sorrel horse, there was too much new to see, a sudden freedom to glory in. There was no time to waste in looking back.

I had come prepared, or thought I had. A gunsmith had reworked my longrifle, making it like new. On my left hip I wore a big cast-steel knife the gunsmith had fashioned, a heavy thing with a hickory handle, a blade two inches wide and fourteen inches long. It was better than a hatchet or a tomahawk for a man in the wilds, the smith had said. I also had a small skinning knife, worn on a belt slung over my shoulder, with a sack of flints and newly-cast lead bullets.

The wagon lumbered along slowly, for its bed sagged with the weight of things we would use in the new land. If left to my own choice, I would have preferred to travel light, perhaps taking a steamboat down the Mississippi to New Orleans, then going by ship to the coast of Texas. Many emigrants were doing it that way. But Pa had argued that this would land us in Texas with only such goods as we could pack. Wagons, plows and other implements would be hard to come by in Texas, and the price would be high.

To be sure, the wagon would slow our trip. It would mean back-straining labor and galling delay in time of rain, or in passing through the pine forests and the dense cane-brakes which lay ahead.

"But," Pa had reasoned, "it'll be all yours when you get there. You'll have the wagon and the horses. You'll have a plow apiece, and an anvil and tools. You'll have saddles and harness and plantin' seed. Two cows, a heifer and a bull. Costs money, Josh, to ride a boat. This way you can live off the country, and so can your stock. What money you've got will still belong to you when you get to Texas."

Two strong gray workhorses pulled the wagon, horses that would be worth a-plenty when they got to where they were going. The cows plodded along with infinite bovine patience at the end of their ropes behind the wagon, udders swinging like the pendulum of a clock. Alongside them walked the heifer, and a big bull calf that we were counting on to sire us a herd in Texas.

We would suffer for this burden on the trip, but we would be better equipped than most folks when we finally crossed the Sabine River into Stephen F. Austin's promised land.

We hadn't gone two miles before we saw a man walking down the road in front of us, an old rifle in one hand and an old canvas bag slung over his shoulder. A spotted hound trailed behind him. It stopped and barked at the wagon. The man turned and smiled broadly. He set the bag down and waved, standing in the road until the wagon drew up almost to him. Then he stepped aside.

"Howdy, Josh. Howdy, Thomas. You-all on your way to Texas?" Muley Dodd waited until we answered yes. Then he said, "I'm on my way to Texas, too."

Feeling pity, I swung down from my horse. "Muley, it's a far piece to Texas. You can't go there thataway."

"I got lots of time, Josh. I got grub in the sack, and powder and lead."

The hound came up and licked my hand. It startled me, and I jerked my hand away. "Muley, you don't have enough supplies in that sack to get you to the Notchy country even, much less to Texas."

"I won't go hungry. I can follow bees. Besides, I got money, too. I got three dollars and fifty-two cents." Eagerly Muley reached into his pocket. "Here, I'll show you."

I shook my head and glanced at Thomas as if to ask him what to do. "Muley, you got to go on back home."

"I already left home. Ain't got no folks there no more, and the roof's about to fall in on that old shack anyhow. I'll built me a real pretty house when I git to Texas."

I motioned for Thomas to get down off the wagon and walk with me out to the side of the road. "Thomas, what we goin' to do about Muley?"

"Nothin'. He's not our responsibility."

"He's not *nobody's* responsibility. He's got no folks."

"You've taken care of him for years, Josh. Now let somebody else do it."

"When Muley gets a notion in his head, he don't turn away from it. If he's got it in his mind to go to Texas, he'll keep walkin' till he dies!"

"You fixin' to tell me we ought to take him with us? If you are, you'll just be wastin' your breath."

Thomas climbed back onto the wagon seat. "Goodbye, Muley," he said, and set the team to moving again.

Muley waved good-naturedly. "Good-bye, Thomas. I'll see you in Texas."

I stared at Muley, worried and a little impatient. Thomas was right: I shouldn't have to be saddled with Muley all my life. Something came to me out of the Bible, something about the faith of the mustard seed. Muley had no conception of what lay ahead of him. But he had plenty of faith.

Muley said, "Thomas is fixin' to go off and leave you, Josh. You better catch up. I'll see you-all again when I get to Texas."

I rode on ahead, catching up to the wagon. But I couldn't keep from looking back. And Muley Dodd kept coming. Sometimes I could hear him whistling at the dog. Finally I said, "Thomas, you'd just as well stop. I'm not goin' without Muley."

All my life I had heard tell of the Mississippi River, but I wasn't prepared. There it stretched in front of us, its lazy brown waters so wide that the river was almost scary to look at. The first money we had spent since leaving home, we spent for passage across on a ferry. It was a long, slow crossing. The ferry heaved, and so did Muley Dodd.

Finally, when we pulled the wagon down onto the west bank and paused to look back across the Big Muddy, I caught for the first time the full sense of parting. It touched me deeper than I expected. Crossing this river was like turning a page in a book. Distance was a relative thing, but a barrier like this was something real, something we could see. It was like shutting a door behind us, knowing we might never cross this river again. It was a sobering thought, as long as it lasted. But it didn't last long. There was a camp to be made, and fresh meat to be hunted.

Crossing Louisiana, we were held up for days by hard spring rains which bogged the wagon to the hubs in black mud that gave way so easily to the iron-rimmed wheels but yielded them up so grudgingly. This was a place where even Thomas was glad to have Muley along. Being as little as he was, Muley had a strong back. He thrived on hard work, as long as somebody told him what to do.

Hunting was poor. Camp meat ran low. We went deeper than we had intended into our supply of ground corn. Muley's own sack had long since run out of grub, so there was a third mouth to feed. But even if we went hungry we would not touch the sack that carried the seed corn, a tough strain that had served the Buckalew family well in Tennessee and would see us through in Texas.

I whiled away the idle hours by studying a map of Texas until I had it memorized in every detail. Muley spent time with his spotted hound, which he had named Hickory, after Andrew Jackson. Muley tried to rename him Texas, but the hound wouldn't answer to it, so finally it was Hickory again.

A friendly sun came out at last to harden the soaked earth. We greased the axles afresh and started the wheels turning once more. Much of the country we crossed now was wild, and we traveled long distances without seeing much sign of people. Some movers would have been tempted to stop here and settle, for it appeared there was plenty of room. But not the Buckalew. We were men of tradition. We always went the whole way.

At length we came out of the thick pine timber to the Louisiana Creole town of Natchitoches, on the right bank of the Red River. This was the jumping-off place for Texas-bound overland travelers. About 120 miles west, across the Sabine River, waited the ancient Spanish settlement of Nacogdoches, the easternmost town in Mexican Texas. It was here in Natchitoches that Stephen F. Austin had disembarked from a steamboat in June of 1821 to make his first trip into that vast expanse of alien country where his father, the late Moses Austin, had dreamed of a rich American colony and a recovery of lost family fortunes.

The Creoles by now were used to travelers, finding them a profitable source of trade. They got little from the Buckalews. Thomas held the purse strings with a tight-clamped hand. What we didn't really need, we would do without. What we did really need, we had brought with us.

"Just a final little jolly, Thomas," I cajoled. "This is our last chance in the United States. Be a sport."

Thomas was resolute. "I've never *been* a sport. You want to dance? Dance around that there wagon and grease the hubs."

I didn't argue with him much. Even if Thomas had been open handed with me—an unlikely development—I wouldn't have spent more than the price of a jug. The weeks of hard, slow travel on dim trails and the painful care we gave our cargo had sobered me considerably. I could understand and respect the responsibility my brother carried.

"Then I reckon me and Muley will go look around some. See what these here French folks have got to offer."

"You watch out," Thomas said sternly. "Don't be gettin' in no fights over Muley. Somebody acts like they're
goin' to pick on him, you just bring him on back to the
wagon. No arguments."

"No arguments," I promised.

We had hardly left the wagon when we saw the four
horsemen. They rode toward the camp in a slow walk,
stopping to peer curiously at the wagon from thirty or
forty yards.

Muley caught my arm. "Josh, what kind of men you
reckon them fellers are?"

"I don't rightly know." Two of them were a lot like
the type I had known in the Tennessee settlements all
my life—outdoorsmen with sun-browned, tangle-bearded
faces. The floppy hats, the homespun shirts, the woolen
breeches were familiar enough.

The other two were different, and I guess my mouth
was open as I stared at them. They were both small and
wiry, hungry-looking. Their faces were dark, but not the
same as those of the Negroes back in Tennessee. They
wore peculiar hats with tall, pointed crowns and the wid-
est brims I had ever seen. One had an embroidered black
vest that must have been something special once, though
now it was dirty and threadbare. Both men wore leather
breeches and boots, and spurs with huge, wicked rowels.
One of them spoke to the other, and the words were
foreign. They made no sense to me.

Mexicans, I realized. Yonder, to the west, sprawled the
huge Republic of Mexico. It was natural that we might
encounter Mexicans here, the first we had ever seen. The
strangeness of the men made us hold still in wonder and
keep our silence.

At length the four rode closer. One man nodded with
some show of friendliness. "Howdy, friends." His teeth

were stained from tobacco. "Be you-all headin' for Texas?"

I found myself picking up his manner of speaking. "Yes, sir, we be."

"Where do you-all come from?"

"Tennessee."

The man glanced at his companions. "Hear that, Foley? They be homefolks."

I couldn't keep my eyes from the Mexicans. "*They* ain't from Tennessee."

The man said, "Foley and me, we left Tennessee a mighty long time ago. Miguel and Alfredo, of course, they don't know Tennessee from Massachusetts. They be Meskin."

Excitement stirred in me. I asked the nearest Mexican, "You come from Texas?"

The Mexican glanced at the Tennessean who had done the talking. The Tennessean said. "You got to pardon Miguel. He don't know much English, 'cept a few words like *eat* and *sleep* and *women*."

I felt an awe of these strange men. "You mean you know how to talk *their* language?"

"Sure. You learn it easy when you git to Texas. All you need is a good teacher—a good-*lookin'* teacher."

I grinned at Muley. "It's real lucky, us runnin' into these fellers. They can tell us a right smart that we ought to be a-knowin'." I looked back at the men. "My name's Joshua Buckalew. Just Josh, is all I use. This here is Muley Dodd."

The big man leaned forward in the saddle and took my hand. "I answer to 'Lige'. For Elijah, you know, like in the Book. He was one of them prophets, or maybe it was a disciple—I forgit which. That there is Foley. The Meskins, they got names longer than a hoe handle, but all you need to remember is Miguel and Alfredo. How many with you, Josh?"

"Just us and my brother Thomas. Us three is all."

The man frowned, looking toward the wagon. "Sure got a load of plunder, just for three of you."

"We figured to be prepared. Come meet my brother." I turned and walked ahead. I shouted, "Thomas, come see what's here."

Thomas came around the wagon, halted and stared, a sharp question in his eyes.

I said, "These fellers come from Texas."

Thomas's eyes seemed to harden as his gaze drifted from one to the other. "How do."

His unfriendly manner caught me by surprise. "Thomas, I said they come from Texas. There's a lot they can tell us."

"I already been told a right smart."

For a moment Lige seemed to stiffen. Then he eased again. "How long before you figger on leavin', Thomas?"

Thomas shook his head. "Can't say for certain. Might stay a spell."

That was a lie, for we had planned to leave the next morning. But I held my silence.

Lige rubbed his beard. "Your brother's a cautious man, Josh. And he's right. It don't pay to trust strangers in these parts. Man can't be too careful in a new country." He took a long last look at the wagon and the livestock. "Fine outfit you got. You ought to git off to a good start in Texas." He pulled his horse around. Foley and the two Mexicans followed his example.

I called, "Maybe we'll see you again. There's a heap of questions I'd like to ask."

Lige replied over his shoulder, "Any time, Josh."

When they were gone, I turned angrily on Thomas.

"If you'd been civil we could of talked with them. You wasn't like this at home!"

"We ain't at home, Josh."

"But they was homefolks, and they been in Texas."

"Just because a man's from Tennessee don't mean he's gospel-honest." Thomas frowned. "You're in a strange country, Josh. You don't trust nobody till you have time to size them up. And you don't go tellin' anybody what your plans are. Remember that!"

"They been on the trail. You condemned them because of what they looked like."

"Some things, Josh, you learn to take by instinct. Out in the woods, did you ever sense a varmint before you seen it? It was like that with them four. It was like I had come across a pack of wolves. Nothin' you can put a finger on, but the feelin's there. And when it's there, I pay heed to it."

"I didn't get that feelin'."

"It'll come to you. And till it does, we'll go by my instincts."

That should have been the end of it, for Pa had pledged me to follow Thomas in all important things. But I still burned to find out about the country we were heading for. I wouldn't exactly go looking for Lige. But if we should happen to come across him by accident. . . .

Muley and I started to resume our walk down to the town. Thomas said, "Don't you be late. We want to get started by daylight."

Trailed by Muley's spotted hound, we walked up and down the length of the town, pausing to stare at the river, looking at the small boats, listening with a keen ear to the strange Creole talk.

I shook my head. "I expect it means as much to them as English means to us."

Muley said in all innocence, "I don't understand English neither. I just talk American."

"That's not what I mean. Muley. It's just that . . ." I broke off, for there was no explaining to Muley. I wasn't even sure I understood it all myself. Take for instance the name of the town: *Natchitoches*. Anybody could look at the word and see how it was supposed to sound. But these people called it something like NAK-i-tosh. I figured either the people who had named the town hadn't been able to spell, or the people who lived here now just didn't know how to read.

Muley wasn't satisfied. "Those little kids yonder, how are they supposed to know what they're talkin' about?"

I just shrugged.

Muley said, "Looks to me like it would be simpler if everybody in the world just got together and decided to talk like *we* do. It must be the best language anyhow, or they wouldn't of wrote the Bible in it. Ain't that so?"

"I expect."

"Looks like it sure would save everybody a heap of bother."

After a couple of hours of looking around, we hadn't seen anything of the four men. We figured they had left town. Then on our way back to Thomas, we stumbled right into their camp. We found ourselves facing them over the flicker of a dying fire. I sensed a vague hostility. "Let's move in closer, Muley. They probably can't tell who we are."

Lige took a couple of steps forward, hand on a pistol stuck in his waistband. Then he smiled. "Well, I'll swear it's the lads from Tennessee. Set down here, Josh, you and Muley. Share some poor vittles with us. We got a little left."

I looked around for their wagon and saw that they had none. There were only four saddle horses and a couple of pack animals, staked out on the grass. "Thanks, but we wouldn't want to put you out none. We'd drink a little coffee, though, if you got any." We'd been using ours sparingly because we knew it would be expensive in Texas.

"Sure," said Lige, all friendship and smiles. He spoke in Spanish. Miguel fetched a jug. Lige said, "Before the coffee, a little drop of kindness. For Tennessee, and fond recollections."

Muley drank first and went into a coughing fit. Then I tipped the jug over my arm. Whatever it was, it felt as if it would burn a hole plumb through me.

Lige said, "That's Meskin stuff, pretty hot doin's. Not as good as old Tennessee makin's, but it don't lack for authority."

I gasped, "That's for certain sure."

The burn was a while in wearing off. I didn't care for another. Lige laughed as I blinked the tears from my eyes. Muley still coughed a little, trying to clear his throat. It came to me that Foley and the Mexicans were staring at us, their eyes hard. All of a sudden I didn't like these men. Lige was probably all right, but the others . . .

Even disliking them, I kept glancing at the Mexicans. And Muley stared at them in honest curiosity.

"Lige," I said, "I want you to tell us about Texas."

Lige shook his head. "It's a mighty big subject."

"Just the important things, what we ought to know before we get there."

Lige shrugged. "Well, if I was givin' advice, I'd say the thing most emigrants do wrong is to come unprepared. But from the looks of your wagon, you-all come loaded for bear. So the next thing is to decide where you want to settle."

"We talked to a Colonel Ames back home. He said we

could get land in Austin's colony. You know Colonel Ames?"

Lige frowned. "Can't say as I recollect the gentleman. I know Austin, though."

Foley hadn't spoken before. Now he put in bitterly: "Everybody knows abut the good Colonel Austin. Him and his damned whip."

That surprised me. "I thought everybody liked Austin."

Lige replied quickly, "Most folks do. Foley there, he's got a personal grudge is all, and he talks too much." He frowned at Foley. "Austin is pretty much the whole law in his colony. A man who strays off of the straight and narrow has got to answer to Austin. He's a little feller, and he looks gentle, But now and again he rears up and shows his teeth. Now, Foley had a friend who done a transgression, and Austin ordered the man whipped and throwed out of the colony. Foley ain't forgave that."

My flesh crawled. "Whippin' *is* an awful salty punishment."

"It beats hangin'. They can't hang a man in Texas lessen they git permission first out of Saltillo, and that's way to hell south. Takes a long time. So usually they just whip a man out of the settlement and hope somebody else'll hang him. They don't appreciate the rough element in Austin's colony."

Lige paused as if a sudden thought had come to him. "By the bye, you'll be needin' to be able to show you're of good character. *I* can tell by lookin', but Austin sets a heap of store in seein' it wrote down."

"Thomas and me, we got letters from Colonel Ames and some of the quality folks around home. And *we'll* vouch for Muley."

"It takes a little money, too, to pay down on the land. I hope you got money."

A warning tingle of suspicion touched me. I had never traveled before, but it seemed unlikely to me that quality folks would ask a man if he was carrying money. Muley spoke up with enthusiasm. "Sure, they got money. *I* got money, too." He reached in his pocket for it. "I got three dollars and fifty-two cents."

I said, "Muley!"

Lige grinned. "That's good, Muley. That much money'll take you a long ways in Texas." Lige reached into the fire for a burning stick and used it to light his pipe. His eyes fastened onto me, and I began feeling uncomfortable. "You know somethin', lad? I like you two. Yes, sir, I like you. And I'm fixin' to give you a mite of advice. Between here and Texas there's a heap of unpleasant things layin' in wait for the unwary. You got to cross the Redlands. Lots of hard characters in there. Some been run out of the colony and don't dare go back to the States. Others been run out of the States and can't go to Austin's. So they just squat in the Redland and turn their hands to mischief. Dangerous for three young fellers alone with one wagon."

I sipped his coffee and hoped my eyes did not betray the suspicion that was boiling up in me. "We'll do all right."

"Been others felt that way and never got to Texas alive."

I made no reply.

Lige said, "You need to join up with others a headin' for Texas. We'll be goin' that direction ourselves pretty quick. We'd be right tickled to have you with us."

My gaze drifted from one man to another. The eyes of Foley and the Mexicans were cold. And so was my back.

Foley was twisted sideways, his right arm bent awkwardly as he tried to scratch along his spine. The truth came to me like the flash of a pineknot exploding in a campfire: Foley's back was sore. It wasn't a friend of Foley's who got whipped out of the colony. It was Foley himself!

Suddenly cold all over, I spilled what coffee was left in the cup and pushed to my feet. "We'll see about it." I handed Lige the cup. "Thomas and me, we decided to camp close by here for a week or so and rest up the stock. We'll think on what you said."

It was a lie, but I hoped they wouldn't sense that.

Lige said, "We'll come around and see you in a few days."

As we walked back to our own camp, Muley protested, "I thought Thomas said we was goin' to leave early in the mornin'. It's a sin to lie. How come you lied, Josh?"

I didn't answer him. At the wagon Thomas sat back from the fire, a plate in his hand. He was impatient. "You been gone a long time."

"We ran into those men who stopped at our wagon today, the ones who said they were from Tennessee."

Thomas's eyes narrowed, but he didn't say anything. "Remember what you told me about bein' able to smell a varmint?"

"I remember."

"Well, I think I smelled *four* of them."

Thomas went back to eating. It was several minutes before he said anything, though I thought I saw satisfaction in his eyes as I told him all there was to tell. At length Thomas remarked, "Four men like that wouldn't have much trouble killin' two, would they?" He glanced at Muley. "Or *three?*"

I shook my head. "Not when the three thought the four were friends."

Thomas nodded. "You're smartenin' up, Josh. Tonight we'll get the wagon ready. Come sunup, we'll be three hours down the trail."

Chapter Three

We had a map drawn by Colonel Ames, but we found it more useful to follow wagon tracks and tree blazes than to depend upon the map for more than the most general type of guidance. Looking back over our shoulders every so often for sign of Lige and his three partners, we traveled three days through a black-soil country that looked as if it would take only a little spit to turn it into a quagmire.

The third night the rain started. It was still raining at daybreak when we hitched the team. The wagon moved ten feet and sank halfway to the hubs.

Thomas accepted it philosophically with no more than a shrug of his shoulders and a frowning glance at the heavy timber just behind us. "If we got to bog down, let's do it out in the open where we can see what's comin' around us."

We hadn't spoken to Muley of our suspicions. Muley

was like a little boy—easily made happy and easily frightened. No use frightening him now, for he was having a good time.

"You reckon they'll still come?" I asked Thomas.

"They might, if they don't find better pickin's in Natchitoches. I got a feelin' this bunch of cutthroats wouldn't be choosy."

So we fought the wagon out into the open. I tied the sorrel on with the team and used him to help pull while Thomas and Muley threw their shoulders against the mired wheels and pushed. The spotted dog now and again would bark at the straining team as if trying to do his bit. By midmorning we were two hundred yards out into the clear.

"We'll stop now." Thomas said, his chest heaving from exhaustion, rain spilling from the flattened brim of his mud-streaked hat.

We staked the livestock on grass close by and stretched an extra wagonsheet out from one side of the wagon to give us a place where we could stay out of the rain. This precaution came late, for we were already soaked. We huddled over a small fire which was kept alive with dry wood save inside the wagon.

No one came that day. In the night Thomas and I took turns sitting up on watch. We couldn't trust Muley to stay awake. Next morning the rain stopped. The sun came out from behind the breaking clouds to raise steam from the black, sodden ground. The second day of sunshine we hitched up and made a try. We moved a hundred feet and quit.

"If they come," said Thomas, "at least we're in a position to see them before they get here."

And they came. The four horsemen emerged from the timber in late afternoon. Lige rode in the lead. They halted, seeing the mired wagon in the open. Lige came riding on cautiously, Foley and the two Mexicans trailing by a length or so. They left two pack horses behind.

Thomas was dozing. I touched him gently. "Thomas they've come."

He was awake instantly, reaching for his rifle. I saw Muley off in the grass, running with the hound.

"Muley," I yelled, "come here, quick! Run!"

Muley caught the urgency in my voice. He saw the four men and came sprinting. "They Indians, Josh? They Indians?"

"No, Muley, not Indians. But help me bring the stock in and tie them to the wagon. We don't want them run off."

Muley did as he was told. He asked no questions, though his frightened eyes showed a-plenty of them. We tied the team and the milk cows securely. Picking up my rifle, I said, "Muley, you stay right here, tight by the wagon. Don't say nothin' and don't do nothin'."

Thomas stood ten feet out from the wagon, his rifle cradled over his left arm. I joined him.

Lige reined up. He eyed us critically. Finally he said, "I wouldn't noways call this friendly."

Thomas's voice was cold. "Neither would I."

Foley reined up on one side of Lige. The Mexicans stopped on the other. Their eyes were hostile.

Lige made a show of disappointment. "A man would have to take this as a sign of distrust. You must think we're robbers or somethin'."

I replied, "The thought did occur to us."

"Here I been tellin' Foley and the boys that you-all just changed your minds and left Natchitoches a little earlier than you intended to. If I was of a suspicious nature, I might think you just plain lied to us."

Thomas said, "We don't want trouble. You-all just ride on by us and don't be a stoppin'."

Lige's eyes began to harden. "If we *was* robbers, you boys would be in a tough spot now. I judge that you still can't move that wagon. That boy yonder . . ." he pointed at Muley, "ain't goin' to be of no use to you, so it'd be just you two against us four. And you got just one shot apiece."

Thomas's voice was flat. "We'd make those two shots count. You don't know which two we'd kill."

Lige glanced at his companions. "We come to do these boys a favor and see how it turns out! The milk of human kindness has done clabbered."

Foley scowled. "It's a long way to Texas. They got to sleep sometime."

Thus was all pretense stripped away. Lige shed his false friendliness like a shabby old coat. He looked at the wagon with unmasked greed, plainly calculating what it and its contents would sell for in Texas.

"Boys," he said, "there ain't no use you-all dyin' for this. You can always git you another wagon someday. But once you're dead, nobody can bring you back to life till the Angel Gabriel hisself blows on that horn."

I said, "We ain't dead yet."

"And you needn't be, boy, you needn't be. Think it over. We'll be back in the mornin'. You just ride out in the nighttime and forgit you ever seen us, or that you ever had a wagon."

Lige pulled his horse around and started back to the timber. Foley and the Mexicans held a moment, their hostile eyes fixed on us and our rifles. They had expected to ride directly into camp and have the whole thing over within a moment of complete surprise.

One of the Mexicans spat something in Spanish that I didn't understand. But the other was clear enough when he drew his forefinger across his throat. The three men reined around and went off after Lige.

I just stood there, my hands frozen on the rifle. Muley began whimpering, "Josh, what do them fellers want? Josh. I don't think I like them fellers."

I licked my dry lips. "Thomas, what comes next?"

Thomas shook his head. He lowered his rifle. "Depends on *them*. Like as not they'll lay up yonder in the timber and snipe at us. Let's don't be makin' them a target."

"Like Foley said, it's a long trail to Texas. We can't dodge bullets the whole way."

Thomas shook his head again. "No, we can't. So we'll just lay low and see what kind of move they make."

"What if they don't make one?"

"Then we will."

Muley trembled, and it took all the persuasion I could muster to get him settled down.

Every time one of us stepped out into the clear, a rifle ball would buzz like an angry hornet. The first one bothered me considerably. The second one made me mad. "What do they want to do that for? They can't hit us at this range."

"They might," Thomas said, "if they're lucky. Mostly they want to keep us stuck here till they can pick their own time to come and get us. And maybe they think they can scare us into runnin' away and leavin' it all. That's what they want."

"Well, they're scarin' poor Muley to death, and me too, a little bit. All that friendly talk, sweet as sorghum molasses, and then they want to rob us."

The sun went down. I wasn't too hungry, and Muley was so frightened he never even thought of supper. But Thomas was calm. He built up the fire a little and went about heating some leftover rabbit stew. I got the idea somehow that Thomas might even be looking forward to the inevitable conflict with a certain enjoyment.

I made Muley eat, hoping some hot food in his stomach might make him feel better. I forced myself to eat a little, too, though I had no taste for it. As darkness came, the glow of a campfire showed in the timber.

"Eatin' theirselves a good supper," I said with some bitterness.

Thomas only nodded.

"They could stretch this for days if they wanted to," I complained. "And all we can do is sit here."

Thomas's jaw jutted. "Wrong, Josh. That's *not* all we can do." He stared intently at me. "So far, Josh, what fightin' you've done has been of a piddlin' variety. You've fought at the wrong time and in the wrong places for the wrong things. But a bloody nose or a split lip was the worst you could get. Are you ready to fight now when you *could* get a bullet in your gut?"

"Just try me!"

"Way I see it, they either plan on lettin' us sit here and worry all night, or they'll wait till late and try to catch us asleep. Either way, they'll figure *they're* the hunters. I doubt they'll look for us to come huntin'."

"You mean we're goin' after *them*?"

"It sure beats waitin', and our chances are better. Once it turns pure dark, we got a little time before the moon comes up. We can be on them before they know it."

"I'm willin' to try it. But what about Muley? He'll be hindrance to us, not a help."

"*That*," Thomas said sharply, "I tried to tell you in Tennessee. But anyhow, he stays here."

"He'll be scared."

"He'll stay if we have to tie him. You tell him that!"

We checked our rifles. Each of us loaded a cap-and-ball pistol. Two weapons apiece meant a total of only four shots, with four targets. That was drawing it mighty fine. If four shots failed to do the job, each of us still wore a wicked Arkansas toothpick strapped to our belts, a heavy hunting knife with razor-sharp blade of cast steel.

Muley watched our preparations wide-eyed. "What you fellers fixin' to do, Josh?"

"We're goin' huntin' in a little while. Don't fret, Muley."

We smothered the fire, then sat awhile in the darkness, listening. In the timber we could still see the glow of the robbers' camp. Worriedly I whispered, "How do we know they won't be comin' after *us*, and we won't run into them in the dark someplace?"

"We don't. We just have to go on faith and hope, and depend on them not bein' in no hurry. You scared?"

I started to say I wasn't, but it would have been a poor lie. "If I was any scareder I'd have to change breeches."

Thomas said, "Well, it's about as dark as it's goin' to get. We want to be in the timber before the moon comes up. You talk to Muley, and be sure that dog of his is tied to the wagon."

Muley trembled. "You leavin' me here by myself, Josh?"

"Just for a little while, Muley. You got to stay and look after the stock. Don't you leave this wagon for nothin' , you hear me? Don't leave it at all."

Muley was dubious. "I ain't goin' to like it here, Josh."

"You stay, though. Don't leave it for a minute, or I'll be real mad at you."

"I don't want you bein' mad at me, Josh."

"Then you mind what I tell you."

We moved out, our soft-leather moccasins noiseless on the wet earth. I stayed close to Thomas, for I could hardly see even the outline of him in the darkness. If we ever strayed twenty feet apart, we would lose each other.

We crouched low and moved softly, pausing often to drop to our knees and listen. Hearing nothing but the night birds and the crickets, we would move on a way, then stop again. Back at our wagon, we heard the dog set in to barking. For an awful minute or two I thought the robbers might be stalking Muley. But the barking stopped. Presently we were in the edge of the timber. Ahead, brighter now, glowed the campfire. We paused again to listen. This time we heard voices.

We nodded at each other, satisfied that the four men were still in camp. Thomas signaled for me to follow him. Cautiously, testing the ground each time we put a foot forward, we moved toward the fire.

Thomas's outline showed against the dim glow, bent low and edging in close. Soon we were in the fringe timber around the clearing where the outlaws had made their camp. Without looking back, Thomas hand-signaled me to come up beside him. We knelt to watch, and to consider.

Nearest us, at perhaps twenty feet, Foley sat with a jug, scowling. "I say we ought to've took them, Lige. How do we know they ain't packin' up right now and movin' out?"

Lige stood beyond the fire, thumbs hooked in the waistband of his woolen breeches. "They'd just bog that wagon. I say let them sweat a little. They'll be easier handled when they git good and scared. A scared man don't generally shoot good."

One of the Mexicans sat silently with a long dirk in one hand and a whetstone in the other. The steel blade made a whispering sound each time it passed over the stone. At length the Mexican pulled up a runner of winter-dried grass, left from the previous fall. He slashed at it. The runner floated back to earth in two pieces. The

Mexican nodded his satisfaction and said something in Spanish.

The other Mexican lay stretched out on a blanket, evidently asleep. A small jug sat beside him.

I looked for their weapons. Foley's rifle lay on the ground within easy reach. The Mexican Miguel held the dirk. I couldn't see how the sleeping Mexican was armed. So far as I could tell, Lige had no weapon on him. He was twelve or fifteen feet from any rifle in view.

Thomas whispered in my ear, "Rifles first. I'll take Foley. You take the Mexican that's got the knife. We'll have to get Lige and the other Mexican with our pistols."

"Just shoot them? From ambush?"

"That's what they would've done to us!"

The rifle hammers clicked loud and metallic in the night air. Foley and Miguel jumped to their feet. Foley moved so rapidly I hardly saw him bring the rifle up. In the split second between the flash in the pan and the roar of my rifle, the Mexican sent the dirk spinning toward me. I saw him stagger. Then the blade slashed into my arm.

Thomas made his shot good. Foley's rifle dropped harmlessly to the ground.

The other Mexican was awake instantly, groping desperately for a weapon and tipping over his jug. Thomas dropped his rifle and drew the pistol out of his waistband. The pistol flashed, and the Mexican fell.

Across the fire, Lige stood stunned. He made no move toward a weapon. The nearest was too far for him to reach. He turned and ran into the night.

Thomas shouted, "Shoot him, Josh, quick!"

But I was swaying, the warm blood running down my arm. Instinctively I reached up and pulled the dirk out. I stood with it in my hand and stared in blind shock at the dead Miguel.

Thomas leaped forward, grabbed up Foley's rifle and fired it into the darkness. But he missed, for we could hear Lige's footsteps and the man's heavy body, crashing through the timber.

Thomas stepped back into the firelight and methodically began to reload his pistol. Pursuit would be useless. "Why didn't you shoot him, Josh?" Then he noticed for the first time that I was wounded. "Josh, I didn't know. How bad did he get you?"

I shook my head. "It's bleedin'. That's all I can tell."

Thomas led me closer to the fire for a better look. "It's risky, us bein' close to the fire this way. But I don't expect Lige got away with a gun. He'd of used it already."

My stomach turned over. "Look out, Thomas. It's all coming up."

And it did. But afterward I felt better. Thomas bound the wound tightly, and the bleeding stopped.

We heard footsteps again, a man running. Thomas pulled me away from the fire and into the darkness. He held the reloaded pistol ready.

"Josh!" a voice called excitedly. "Josh! Where you at, Josh?"

"It's Muley," Thomas said. "I knew he wouldn't stay at the wagon."

"He stayed till it was over with. That was the main thing."

Thomas called, "Over here, Muley."

Muley came into the firelight, his eyes wide. He shrank back when he saw the bodies.

"It's all right. Muley." I said. "We got them before they could get us."

Shakily Muley asked, "They all dead?"

"I reckon."

Getting braver. Muley moved close to look. He

pointed to the Mexican who had been caught asleep. "This one ain't dead. Josh. He's movin'."

The wounded Mexican had inched himself along on the ground until he had reached a knife. His fingers were closing around it when Thomas leveled the pistol. A faint smile came to my brother's face. The pistol flashed. The Mexican's fingers spread and dug into the mud. Then they went stiff.

A chill ran all the way down to my boots. I stared hard at Thomas, for this was something I had never seen in him before.

Thomas caught the look. "It had to be done."

"You didn't have to enjoy it."

"Was that how it looked?"

I nodded. Thomas said, "I didn't. But on the other hand, I can't say as it bothered me none, either."

From far off we heard a horse running. I knew without having to see. "It's Lige! He's stolen one of our horses."

Thomas swore.

Thinking about it, I shrugged. "Well, maybe it was a fair trade. He couldn't get to his own. We lost one horse but got six."

Thomas shook his head. "No, Josh. We'll pick the best one from theirs to replace the one we lost. We'll turn the rest of them loose."

My mouth dropped open. "Turn them loose? Thomas, we can use those horses. And it's a cinch *these* men will never need them again."

Thomas shook his head again. "*They're* the thieves, not us. We don't steal, even from dead men."

He had a strange sense of values, my brother did. He could smile while he killed a man. But he wouldn't take that man's horses.

He said, "We'll go back to our own camp now. Come mornin', Muley and me will come over here and give these men a plantin'. I doubt your arm will be in shape for diggin'."

He studied the two dead Mexicans, first one and then the other. "A real pair of cutthroats, weren't they? The first Mexicans we ever saw, and they tried to kill us. Gives us a lot to look forward to when we have to live amongst them in Texas."

"Maybe the others won't be like these. Thomas. These were outlaws."

He didn't even seem to hear me. And if he had, it wouldn't have made any difference. Thomas made his mind up in a hurry. And once made up, it never changed. He grunted. "They're a sorry class of people."

"The other two weren't Mexicans," I argued. "They was from Tennessee."

I had as well have kept my silence. Thomas said, "I told you I could smell them just like wolves. I've already decided one thing, Josh."

"What's that?"

"I'll never trust a Mexican!"

Chapter Four

Among the towering pines at the far eastern edge of Mexican Texas, hardly a horse-lathering ride from the international boundary of the Sabine River, Nacogdoches was the gateway. Once it had been a sleepy Spanish village, site of the Mission Nuestra Señora de Guadalupe, trying to bring the *padres'* message of God to the heathen of the woods. Now it was awake and bustling, the gathering place for hopeful immigrants bound for Texas, and for the wishful ones who had gotten that far on nerve and could go no further. It had also become a gathering place for a lawless element that had been run out of the colonies or never had been able to get in. It was a lonely garrison for Colonel José de las Piedras and a comparative handful of homesick soldiers serving hundreds of miles from the villages of their birth. This ancient Spanish town was legally Mexican now, since

Mexico had broken away from Spain. But in truth it was actually much more American.

Not long before, General Manuel de Mier y Terán had taken a long, painful look and had found Mexican influence all but gone, except that a lax and corrupt municipal government still functioned on old Mexican customs of bribery and self-interest. "The whole population here is a mixture of strange and incoherent parts without parallel in our federation," he had written worriedly. He was right, for criminals from the old Neutral Ground squatted here, along with a scattering of Indians from many tribes, and French and Spanish creoles, genteel American planters and raw frontiersmen.

Terán wanted to shut off the immigration of Americans before the situation became worse.

True, through here had passed filibusters and free-booters beyond counting. Here in 1812 had come the Gutierrez-Magee Expedition to invade Texas when it was still a part of Spain. In 1819 Dr. James Long had marched down from Natchez with 300 men and had held Nacogdoches temporarily. In 1826 one Haden Edwards had received permission from Mexico to settle 800 families in Eastern Texas but found himself unable to evict Mexican and American squatters and Cherokee Indians from the land which had been given him. He and his brother Benjamin established themselves in Nacogdoches' old stone fort and proclaimed the Republic of Fredonia. This republic crumbled quickly in the face of Mexican troops, bolstered by militia which Stephen F. Austin raised. Austin was for law and order. The law happened to be Mexican, and he respected it.

Terán had gotten his law. Except for the Austin and Green DeWitt colonies, legal immigration of these blue-eyed foreigners had all but stopped.

Illegal immigration was another matter.

*   *   *

We Buckalews knew little of this as our wagon groaned
into Nacogdoches. Colonel Ames back in Tennessee had
mentioned that there had been a mite of trouble once or
twice, but he had reckoned it was past history. He had
written a letter for us which Thomas in turn had given
to an Austin representative in Natchitoches. We had been
handed an immigration document with Austin's signature
on it to guarantee us clear passage.

Lige had stolen my sorrel to get away that night in the
timber west of Natchitoches. Now I rode a young bay
gelding which had been Lige's. I had talked Thomas into
letting us keep one more horse for Muley. I still felt he
had made a mistake in turning the other outlaws' horses
loose, but I had to respect his version of what was honest.

Though he sat on the wagon seat beside Thomas, leaning forward eagerly for a view of Nacogdoches, Muley
usually did his talking with me. "Looky yonder what a
town we're comin' to, Josh. Looks like folks is thicker'n
jaybirds at acorn time."

I rode close beside the wagon and nodded, excitement
building in me too. At the Sabine River crossing we had
officially entered Texas, but somehow the feeling wasn't
strong. I couldn't tell that one side of the river looked
much different than the other. I knew it was a foolish
notion, but somehow I had expected the difference to
show right off.

I had expected Nacogdoches to have a Mexican look,
though I had no clear idea what a Mexican look was.
Again I was disappointed, for I saw few people who appeared to be Mexican. Most were light-skinned, like us.
The signs were mostly painted in English.

I had no way of knowing these were the same thoughts
which had bothered General Terán, for at that time I
hadn't even heard of the man. But we were about to be

introduced to the results of Terán's observations.

Thomas's voice was sharp. "Get close to the wagon, Josh. We got company comin'."

Half a dozen horsemen approached, wearing uniforms that had been bright when new but now were faded and wrinkled and browned with grime.

"Didn't expect we'd rate a reception like this," I said.

Thomas frowned. "Raggy-lookin' lot. Mexicans."

He pulled the team to a stop as the soldiers came up. One man circled around and halted beside Thomas, touching his hand to the bill of his cap. His face was a deep brown, his eyes almost black. His uniform had been fancier, once, than the others. He was plainly an officer. His moustache was thick and black, but he was still a young man.

"How do." Thomas said stiffly.

"Buenos días." The Mexican took his time, studying the wagon and the animals trailing it. He spoke, but the words were Spanish and made no sense to us. The Mexican turned in the saddle and called. *"Señor* Charters!"

An American was trailing the soldiers. Astride a fine black horse, he pulled around beside the officer. He gave a courteous nod, exchanged a few words with the Mexican, then turned to us.

"Lieutenant Obregón has not yet mastered the English language. Occasionally I help him. My name is Benjamin D. Charters. I hope I can be of service to you gentlemen."

Thomas was not impressed. "What's he need?" he asked bluntly.

"You gentlemen surely know about the law of 1830, which restricts immigration into Mexico? The lieutenant says he trusts you have some documentary evidence of your right to enter this country."

I studied Charters, trying to discover the reason for

Thomas's quick and adverse judgment. Charters spoke with the ease and eloquence of a lawyer. His suit was cut of good cloth and well-tailored, though it had seen better days. Thin at the knees and elbows, frayed at the cuffs and collar, it told of a genteel poverty.

Thomas reached back into the wagon and got the document with Austin's signature. Charters passed it on to the lieutenant. Obregón read it critically and handed it back, shaking his head.

Charters listened to the officer, then explained, "He says this is not enough. You must have another permit to go beyond Nacogdoches."

Thomas reddened. "They told us in Natchitoches this was all we'd need to get us to San Felipe de Austin."

Charters smiled thinly. "This is a long way from Natchitoches. Some of these garrisons make their own laws."

Thomas's eyes hardened. "What else we goin' to need?"

"You need a new order signed by a local military officer to pass you through the guard at the road to San Felipe."

"How do we get this order?"

"It is difficult, usually. The wait is often very long; you know how slow the military can be about these things. However, the lieutenant says he likes your looks and has decided to do you a favor. He has ways of cutting through regulations when the reason is good enough."

Thomas clinched his fist. "He wants money?"

Charters winked. "A bit of coin is like grease on the wheels of progress. All men have their price. I think you'll find that the lieutenant's price is reasonable."

Thomas was speaking quietly now. I could feel the anger rising in his voice. "What he wants is a bribe."

Charters made a pretense of surprise. "I didn't say

that. Nobody ever bribes anybody in Mexico. This is simply a sort of hidden tax. Everybody pays it when the
occasion arises. They call it *mordida*, the little bite. It is
one of the facts of life in Mexico, like ground corn and
chili pepper."

"What part do *you* get out of it, Charters?"

Charters began to anger. "You are insulting me, sir.
Now, if you don't *want* to go to San Felipe . . ."

"We *are* goin' to San Felipe. And we'll do it without
givin' you or this leather-colored parasite a penny."

"I don't see that you have much choice."

"Tell those Mexicans to get theirselves out of our way
if they don't want to get run over!"

Charters was livid. "This is Mexico. You're a foreigner
here. You'll live up to Mexican laws or suffer the con-
sequences."

"This isn't law, this is a try at robbery. We've been
tried once already, on the way down here. It didn't work
for *them*; it won't work for you."

"Try to move past these men and you'll be stopped."

"You're not gettin' any money out of *us!*"

Charters regained some control. "Look friend, you
could afford to put a little silver across the lieutenant's
palm. The Mexican government doesn't pay these men
much way out here, and what it *does* pay is often slow in
coming. You can't blame these soldiers for taking a little
extra."

"It's wrong. I'll rot here before I'll pay."

Charters spoke to the lieutenant. From his looks I
thought Obregón might order his men to shoot us down
like dogs. I didn't know a word of Spanish then, but I
knew pretty well what kind of language he was spitting
at us. He hadn't learned it in church. He reined his horse
around, savage as an Indian, and signaled his troops to
follow him.

Charters spoke crisply. "You'll get tired of sitting here, and you'll come begging to pay. Obregón will take a very *big* bite then; you can count on that." He rode off, following the troopers.

I thought we had been whipped, but Thomas had a stubborn look of victory all over him.

I said, "Thomas, we're in trouble now. Wouldn't it of been easier to've just paid the man a little somethin'?"

"That would have been a compromise."

"What would that hurt? We always got to compromise!"

"Not when it's right against wrong. If you come to a fork in the road, you got to turn either to the left or the right. You can't compromise. You do what's right, or you do what's wrong. Bribery is wrong, whether it's a dollar or a hundred dollars."

I shrugged. "A man can get awful hungry, tryin' to be right all the time." The soldiers were about out of sight. But they weren't out of mind. "How do we get out of here *without* payin'?"

"There aren't many soldiers. Ever try to stop a creek flowin' by stickin' your hand in it? The water just goes right on, between your fingers. I'll ask around, find out where they guard the trails. Then we'll go the long way around. We don't have to follow *their* route. We'll just make our own!"

Chapter Five

I didn't realize it then, but our encounter with Lige, Foley and the two Mexican bandits, followed by our experience with the hungry Lieutenant Obregón in Nacogdoches had been enough to start hatred to gnawing at Thomas. He had always been one to make up his mind in a hurry. From this time on he had a cold contempt for all things Mexican. Strange, how some people so easily form a hate, and how hard it is for them to find a liking for the new and different.

We did what Thomas said—took the long way around and got clear of Nacogdoches. It was so easy I felt sure there must be a catch to it somehow, but there wasn't. We didn't know that many others had done the same thing before us. We found out later there was a trail which had been used by so many contraband immigrants that it had even won its own name, the Tennesseans'

Road. There just weren't enough Mexican soldiers to patrol the whole country.

As I said, we didn't know this at the time. We thought the idea was original, and we gloried in getting away with it. Not that what we did was illegal in the strict sense. We had the paper from Austin. We had simply avoided having to pay a bribe. But Mexican views of jurisprudence were different than ours. It could have gone hard with us if we had been caught. That's how it was in Mexico in those days. It wasn't the laws written on paper which really counted; it was the men who administered them. In the end, the law was always what they *said* it was.

If written laws were deceptive, so were maps. A mile doesn't look like much on a piece of paper. But on the ground it is something else. The long, long miles passed endlessly beneath the iron-rimmed wheels, and it seemed San Felipe was still a thousand miles away. I had no clear idea of the vast variety of lands we would pass through on the trip—the team; rolling prairies abounding in wild horses and many swamps and marshes that bogged the wagons and exhausted kinds of game; thickets and cane-brakes so dense that once when we strayed off the trail Muley and I had to walk ahead of the wagon and clear a path with axes so Thomas could pick his way through.

As we crossed the map-marked boundary into Austin's colony, we began to come across small settlements and scattered farms. At once we could tell the difference between the legal colony and the squatter element which had prevailed around Nacogdoches. Plainly, Austin had picked these people with a degree of care. Spring-planted crops were coming up in cleared fields which had been virgin grasslands a few months earlier. Log cabins stood along creek banks where Indians had stalked deer or had gathered the native pecans. Wherever we stopped, we found a welcome, for there was a fraternal element in the pioneering experience which made people draw together instinctively. Most of these early colonists were dirt-poor. Their hospitality was almost embarrassing to us, for they would bake us bread from their scant supplies of corn. They would wrap their precious coffee beans in buckskin and beat them with a rock to brew up a drink for us. They were almost pathetic in their eagerness for news of "the States," and we had so little to tell them.

At last we came through a sandy canebrake river bottom to the edge of the broad and lazy Brazos River. Across the river, atop a high bluff on the west side, perched San Felipe de Austin. Situated at the head of navigation, it was the seat of government for most of colonial Texas.

I was disappointed. "That's it? That's all of it?"

Thomas shrugged. "Likely there's more that you can't see on account of the bluff. But I doubt there's really very much. Maybe you been buildin' up too much in your mind."

"I thought it would look Mexican. Log cabins is all I see, the same kind I've seen my whole life long."

Thomas shook his head. "I'd as soon not ever see another Mexican. But they're there, waitin' yonder for us across the river."

I could see them idling at the ferry landing on the other side of the Brazos. An uneasiness started, because I thought this might be where we were going to get caught up with for what we had done at Nacogdoches. But Thomas didn't look worried.

A ferryboat slowly made its way across the river and tied up. Thomas pulled the wagon onto the boat, and we all pitched in to secure it so it wouldn't roll with the motion of the ferry.

The ferryman was one of the swivel-jawed kind. "Sure proud to see young fellers like you-all comin' in. Men of the land. Seems to me like this place has gotten overrun of late with lawyers and the like—soft-handed men. We need more with dirt under their fingernails, the way it was when we first come here with Austin. Yes, sir, I been here pretty near from the first. I was one of Austin's Old Three Hundred. Been a right smart of changes, I can tell you."

I got caught up in his enthusiasm. "It sure is a rich-*lookin'* country, all right. Fish and game like I never saw before. Crops show a heap of promise. And trees—I never knew there was so many different kinds of trees in the whole world."

The ferryman pointed his chin toward the Mexican soldiers raisin' stock. "Sure, we miss the comforts we used to have at home, and we may be a long time ever gettin' most of them. But it's a great country for growin' things. You just drop a seed in the ground and stand back out of the way."

Muley took it for gospel and whistled softly to himself. "I sure do want to see *that!* "

The ferryman pointed his chin toward the Mexican soldiers waiting on the west shore. "You-all got to stand inspection yonder."

"We have the papers," Thomas said, frowning. "The Mexicans give you much bother?"

The ferryman spat. "It ain't that they *do* anything, really; it's just that they're *here,* that's all. Used to, when we first come, we had a right-smart of Indian trouble, and we could've used some soldiers to help us. They wouldn't send any. Now that we're strong enough to take care of our own selves, Mexico sends soldiers in. Maybe they're afraid we've gotten too strong. I get the feelin' sometimes that they're watchin' *us,* not the Indians."

I asked. "If the Mexicans are so worried about us Americans, how come they ever let any of us settle here in the first place?"

"To protect Mexican people from the Indians. Americans always did have a reputation as Indian fighters. Mexico figured to put Americans in between the Indians and their own people. Worked pretty good, too. Many a red devil had died of indigestion on a Texian rifleball."

That was the first time I had heard the word *Texian*. I sensed it was a way the Anglo settlers here spoke of themselves.

The ferryman moved forward as the ferry neared the shore. "Go see Sam Williams over in Austin's land office. He'll introduce you to Austin."

The Mexican soldiers waited as the wagon pulled out onto the river bank. The dislike was plain and open in Thomas's face while a Mexican sergeant came forward to look at the paper. It was easy to see that the black-moustached man couldn't read the words. He was going by the official look of it. But he read the dark look in Thomas's eyes. Rapid Spanish passed back and forth among the ill-clad troops. Not understanding a word of it, I realized for a moment just how helpless and alone an outsider would be. It occurred to me that this was one major barrier between the average Mexican and the average Anglo settler, this difference of language.

"Thomas," I said, "one thing I'm goin' to do as soon as I can is to learn to speak Mexican."

Thomas shook his head. "English is good enough for me."

Muley watched the soldiers with lively interest. "You mean a man can *learn* to talk like they do, Josh? I figured you had to be born with it."

Without friendliness, the sergeant waved us on.

*   *   *

It was more of a town than I had supposed, once we passed through the tall-tree fringe—pecan, oak, ash, cottonwood—and came out over the top of the bluff. There we found a growing settlement situated neatly around an open plaza. It was still a young town, for most of the log buildings had not yet grayed with weathering. The axe-hewn timbers of many houses remained bright and unstained. A few buildings were of rough-sawed lumber, which indicated that somewhere in the region—downriver, we learned later—someone had set up a sawmill.

Thomas pulled the team onto a street that bordered the eastern edge of the plaza. We began to discover that the town was better in appearance than in reality. Like a funeral procession, perhaps, great on length but somewhat thin.

A townsman directed us to Austin's office in one end of a double log cabin, which sat near the bank of a small creek. A moss-strewn oak stood in front of it. A roofed-over open section divided the office from the sleeping quarters. A chimney stood at each end of the cabin.

I was a little let down. "This don't look much like the head office of the whole colony of Texas."

Thomas shrugged. "Handsome is as handsome does. I bet the roof don't leak."

Sam Williams met us at the door. We introduced ourselves. Thomas was of a notion to get right down to business, but he had to hold off until Williams heard all the news we had picked up along the trail. In time, however, Thomas was able to hand him the document with Austin's signature. Williams nodded. "To be sure, you'll be wanting a grant of land. Do you have an idea where you'd like to settle?"

I put in, "We've studied the map till we know it backwards. We'd like to go somewheres west."

Williams' eyebrows arched. "Why west?"

"Why not?" asked Thomas. "You still got land to the west, haven't you?"

"Yes, but it's wilder, farther removed from the more settled portions. It puts you in more danger of contact with Indians. In short, it's a long way to civilization."

Thomas said, "We'll just take civilization with us."

Williams glanced from Thomas to me and back again.

He had sized up Muley in the beginning and paid little attention to him now. "If that's your wish, then, we'll go forward on that basis. You understand about the Mexican colonization laws?"

Thomas replied. "Some. Colonel Ames told us."

"What it amounts to is that a family man can receive a *labor* of farming land and a *sitio* of grazing land if he wants to raise stock. A *labor* is 177 acres. A *sitio* is 4,428."

I whistled. We couldn't get that much land together in two lifetimes back home. Here it was almost handed to us.

Williams went on. "There will be some nominal; fees, of course, for surveying and other costs. I hope you brought enough cash to cover those."

Thomas nodded. "I hope so, too."

"By law, you two brothers as single men won't quality for a full grant each. We can list you as a family, and you can receive that amount together." Williams pointed his chin at Muley Dodd. "How about *him?*"

Muley spoke up eagerly, "I got money for land, too." He dug into his pockets. "I got three dollars and fifty-two cents."

I shook my head. "Muley, that won't be enough. But don't you fret. You can go with us. Whatever we got, you'll have a share of it."

Muley smiled. "Thanks, Josh. You're a good feller, but there's no need. I got my own money. I want to put in my part."

I glanced at Thomas, but he had nothing to say. I shrugged. "If it'll make you happy, Muley. This way, at least, you got a claim on us." My eyes met Thomas's. "Both of us."

As we poured over Williams' maps, we heard a horse trot up to the front of the cabin. A saddle squeaked in thin protest as a man dismounted. Williams glanced through the glassless window. "It's Colonel Austin."

For weeks now, I had been hearing Austin's name. I guess I expected the man to stand eight feet tall. So, for a moment or two as Austin stood in the doorway, I felt the quick sag of disappointment. In reality, Stephen F. Austin was a rather spare man, and he had to lift his face to look at us, even Muley Dodd. He appeared as if he ate irregularly, and not very well. But strength showed in the care-drawn features, and determination in his dark eyes. Only a strong man would ever have dared start the project Austin had fostered here in Texas, much less carry it through this far against all the adversities of nature, human frailty and Mexican law.

Williams made the introductions. I shook hands with a certain amount of awe, for Austin was the only famous man I had ever met. I was surprised at the strength of Austin's grip. Those small hands hadn't looked capable of taking hold so tightly. Williams told about the grant we sought, and Thomas had to explain again—somewhat laconically—why he wanted to settle in the west. Austin read the letter of recommendation from Colonel Ames and several other letters from various people back home in Tennessee. He glanced questioningly at Muley.

"Muley's with us," I said quickly. "We'll vouch for him."

Austin seemed to sense Muley's problem without being told. "This can be a fine country for those willing and able to work. It can be death for the incapable."

"Muley's with us," I repeated.

Austin nodded, dismissing the question as having been answered. "You'll not regret that you've come. Texas is wealthy in natural resources—fertile lands, timber, pasturage. I've seen much of the United States, but I've seen nothing as fine as Texas. Nature has supplied us everything we need except population. You, and others like you, are slowly supplying that." He paused, studying us with those dark, keen eyes. "You are unmarried, I see. Later on, as you marry, you can each obtain enough land to fill out your individual allotment to full size. And, of course, as the children come, we get our population. I might add that if you marry a Mexican woman, the law entitles you to even more land."

Thomas said firmly, "No chance of that."

Austin smiled faintly. "I would wager you've seen no Mexican women yet."

Thomas replied, "We've seen some of the men."

Austin's smile broadened. "You would be surprised how many American men have found Mexican women to marry. Some of them are quite pretty. And they have one sterling qualification: they are *here!*" He let that matter drop and frowned as another thought crossed his mind. "Have you men any strong leanings toward politics?"

Thomas shook his head. "We never been noways connected with politics. The Buckalews have always voted for Andrew Jackson. Past that, we just never was interested."

"I had a good reason for asking. Mexico is still unstable. Governments change like the wind. Politics can be a perilous thing here. I've endeavored from the beginning to keep these colonies free of the political pressures that have been the bane of Mexico. But more and more new men are coming in who will not let matters be. More and more, our people are being caught up in the tides of change. It is a dangerous involvement.

"Out where you're going, you'll have some Mexican neighbors. In many ways you'll find them different from yourselves. In some ways, they are much the same. All humans come from the same mold. Be friendly; get to know them. Accept the differences and be grateful for the things in which you are alike.

"But above all, remain aloof from their politics. They are the natives here, and we are the strangers. Mexico still has turbulent times ahead. It will require a steady hand and a careful silence to see us safely through."

Chapter Six

The surveyor who tied his horse and pack mule behind our wagon and went along with us was a lean, likeable man named Jared Pounce. He had come with the Old Three Hundred, had a farm of his own and did outside work ranging from gunsmithing to surveys. There wasn't much loose money around the colonies, except some counterfeit which floated in periodically from the Redlands. A man did whatever honest work he could that would let him clasp his fingers over a bit of coin.

Pounce liked his tobacco. Wadding a home-grown leaf into one corner of his mouth, he studied the wagon with open admiration. "You lads come prepared. I'll sure grant you that. I been here since almost the first, and I still ain't got me a wagon. There's three classes of settlers in Texas these days. The upper class are them that owns a wagon. The next class down uses a sled. And the lower class, they just have to walk and tote their own load. You lads are startin' off in the upper class."

Now that we were getting near it, I began to itch with impatience for a view of our own land. I begrudged every stop we made. But Pounce wouldn't be hurried along the trail.

"Just take it as it comes, boys. Life's too short to spend it in a lope. There's too much to see and learn and enjoy."

Pounce was a born talker, and we were good listeners, especially when the subject was Texas.

"It's hell on women," Pounce said, "but it's God's own country for a man. You wake up every mornin' to a brand new world, especially when you go west where the people ain't thick yet. There it stands, all around you, as fresh and new as if God had just finished makin' it. Big sky, a whole world of room. Air so fresh that it makes you grow younger instead of older. You never saw such a country for huntin', either. You just step out of your door with a rifle in your hand and there's dinner standin' there waitin' for you. You don't even have to drag it far to the cabin.

"They plan these grants so that they front on the water. You'll want to locate on a clear creek so's to have clear water all the time. The Colorado is a mighty river, but she runs muddy. That's what the name comes from, Mexican for *red*. Man has got to let it settle before he drinks it, or he'll have to lay over to let his stomach settle instead."

Thomas asked, "What about Indians, Jared?"

Pounce squeezed one eye shut and peered off to the north thoughtfully. "They'll bear watchin'. They don't bother folks much anymore in the settlements. But now and again they'll skulk around the fringes and do mischief. You boys'll sure be on the fringe."

Thomas nodded. "Austin said we'd have some Mexicans for neighbors. We apt to have trouble with them?"

Pounce shrugged. "Mexicans have got their own ways. You'll find good ones and bad ones and indifferent, like there is amongst the rest of us. There's saints, and there's sinners. I'd say if you don't bother them, they ain't apt to bother you."

I said, "I reckon a man could even make friends with them."

Pounce replied, "Sure, *I* got some Mexican friends, and I got a few Mexican enemies. It's like anyplace else: you got to judge each man separate. Trust them all and you'll get your fingers burnt. Condemn them all and you'll miss some people that would've been good friends. Out here, you'll need all the friends you can get."

We didn't have to do all our own cooking. Pounce had traveled these trails many times and was acquainted with most of the people. He knew where the good cooks lived. Once he pointed to a low-built log cabin with a half a dozen loose hogs rooted in the front yard. "Always pass up this place here. See the black smoke risin' out of the chimney? That old woman burns everything she cooks. And she ain't none too clean, neither."

He was more likely to refer to people by their cooking than by their names. One place was "the corn-dodger woman's." Another belonged to "the deer-meat and honey man."

Deer and wild turkey were so many it seemed the Lord was being wasteful. We always had something to take to a settler's house along with our appetites. Thomas said he didn't like to receive more than he gave, and I reckoned that was an honest way for a man to be. We noted that, particularly among the newer settlers, meat was the main thing on the dinner table, and wild meat at that. A few of the older colonists usually had bread, made of rough-ground corn. We hadn't seen an egg since Louisiana.

I was careful to study the settlers and their ways of living, for their ways would be our ways. Most—but not all—of the men wore buckskins, the women homespun. The houses were mostly of a kind, built of logs. Some, where the family was large, were big double cabins with an open dog-run in the center. Most of the floors were of earth, though here and there we found a cabin with puncheon flooring. That was a mark of comparative wealth. The windows lacked glass but had shutters that could be opened for air or pulled shut to keep out wind, rain and Indians.

Not everybody had a cabin. At once place we came across a new arrival who hadn't taken time yet to put up any kind of building. He and his wife were still living out of their wagon while they broke the land and got a crop started. There would be a cabin later, when the crop was up.

"That's how it'll be with us, Josh," Thomas said. "We'll likely spend most of this summer sleepin' under the wagon."

"That's what we've done since the day we left home," I said indifferently.

"I like it," Muley put in.

Jared Pounce commented, "Most young men just naturally take to the outdoors. Used to, I could've gone for a year without a roof over my head, and I'd never given it a thought. Now, though, when night comes around I like to look up at the rafters instead of the stars. Sign of age, I reckon."

Time and again we came across grazing bands of wild horses. The best Pounce knew from talking with old-time Mexicans was that these bands had been here for generations. Some said they were descended from horses which had gotten loose or been stolen from Spaniards long ago. Whatever their origin, their reproduction had been remarkable.

"Time or two," said Pounce, "I been reduced to eatin' horsemeat. It ain't so bad, when you got nothin' better to compare by. Some people say it's the heart that rules a man, but they're wrong. It's his stomach."

In due time we hauled up to the Colorado River. As Jared had said, it was red with mud carried in upriver.

"On across," said Jared, "and down to the southwest, is Gonzales. That's the headquarters of the Green DeWitt colony. Above you there's not a lot—a few scattered Americans, some Mexicans. And Indian country."

Standing there, looking out across that muddy river, I felt a deep emotion rolling over me like a flood. I felt a strange joy that I'd never known before, and have never felt again in quite the same way. I sensed that somewhere yonder, not far away now, lay the ground we had been looking for. I knew that soon I would set my boots down on our promised land.

It had been three hours since we had passed the last settler's cabin. We had this all to ourselves. "Thomas," I said. "I got a feelin' about this country. I'm goin' to like it here."

Thomas replied, "We've come too far *not* to like it."

Jared pointed his chin northwards. "Boys, let me make a suggestion to you. One time I was through this neck of the woods on an Indian-chasin' party. Not far from here I came across a place on a creek, as pretty a place as ever I seen. For a long time I kept thinkin' someday I'd come back and take it up. Now I know I never will. It's yours if you want it."

"Show us," Thomas said.

We crossed the river, and we traveled awhile. I knew the place instinctively, even before Jared spoke. I touched spurs to horse and rode ahead across a flat stretch of open ground that one day soon would be a field. Beyond lay an uneven stand of timber along a creek—huge old pecan trees heavy with foliage, rugged live oaks with leaves that would stay green the year around, willow, ash . . . A buck jerked its antlered head toward me, the startled eyes wide and brown. It bounded away into the timber. Three wild turkeys, disturbed by the deer, moved into a trot, then soared at a low level into the shelter of tangled underbrush.

I rode on without slowing until I came to the bank of the creek. Below me was a deep flow of clear water. Looking around carefully for sign of human life and seeing none, I dismounted and tied the horse to a bush. Then, rifle in my hand, I moved down the bank to the water's edge. I tasted it and found it as good as any in Tennessee.

I returned to the flat and waited there, looking around, until the wagon came up. My spirit soared as it had never done before.

"Thomas," I said, "the trip is over. We're home!"

The surveying job took a while. Jared knew his business, but he didn't rush. "This is for ever," he said. "We can't afford mistakes."

Jared would carry his compass. Muley and I took turns carrying the chain, while Thomas stood watch nearby on horseback, the rifle across his lap. Not once was there sign of a human being. It couldn't have been lonesomer if we had staked out a claim on the moon. We had wanted the "far back," and this was certainly it.

When Jared's job was finished and the new claim plainly marked on his map. Muley and I ground some of our scant supply of corn into meal as a gift to him.

"Jared," I asked. "do they ever have elections here in Texas?"

He frowned, not sure of the reason for the question.

"Sure, we elect what we call an *ayuntamiento*, a local government."

I said, "If you ever take a notion to run, let me know. I'll vote for you twice."

He wished us good luck on this land he had wanted so long for himself, as he set out a-horseback, his pack mule trailing. Jared would eat his way back to San Felipe.

We hated to see him go, but there was no time to worry about the isolation, for too much work was long overdue. First thing we did after Jared left was to begin breaking ground on the big flat. It was hot, back-breaking work. Thomas and I took turns standing guard while the other one and Muley strained, sweated and swore behind the heavy wooden plows. We couldn't trust Muley to stand guard. We had tried it, only to see him forget his task and go chasing off with his dog after a rabbit or a deer, or hunting a bee tree.

Weather was hot, and a little on the dry side. With summer on the way, we had to get our seed planted and up to a good stand before the full heat came on, or the corn would wither before it ever made a head. So we kept chopping trees, pulling stumps, breaking ground and putting in seed. It was years and years ago, but I can still remember the rich smell of that fresh-turned earth, opened to the sun after untold ages of darkness.

We didn't allow ourselves to let up from daylight until dark, except for what little time was necessary to hunt game and prepare meals. Thomas was not content with the field. He broke a garden plot near the spot on the creek where we would put up our cabin.

The day finally came when we had caught up, at least temporarily. The corn was rising, and enough rain had fallen so that it would not parch. Now we could begin thinking about a cabin, to get ourselves in from under the wagon. I wanted it closer to the creek, but Jared Pounce had warned us that wherever the wild pecan trees stood, we could expect flooding every so often. Better to tote water an extra distance than to wake up some morning being toted by it.

We built corrals first, for the livestock, and a low-roofed shed open on the south. Then we began felling trees and squaring them up so they would stack and make a neat fit with a minimum of chinking. Because there had been no sign of intrusion, we loosened our reins on Muley, letting him go out after the game it took to keep us fed. Muley was a fair-to-middling shot, though we had to keep warning him about shooting too near the cabin and scaring the game away.

It was Muley who saw the first Indians.

We had begun snaking the finished logs up to the cabin site. Back home we would have made a community celebration out of a cabin-raising, but here there was no community. It was a job we would have to do for ourselves. We had laid the foundation logs and were saddle-notching the first logs for the cabin sides when Muley came running across the flat, shouting all the way. The spotted dog loped along ahead of him. Muley fell once, sprawling face down in the grass. But he was up again in a second, hardly missing a step.

"It's Injuns, Josh! It's Injuns!"

I ran for my rifle. Thomas stood soberly scanning the scattered timber beyond the flat. "I don't see nothin' chasin' him, Josh. You got to remember, Muley ain't bright."

Muley reached us and fell to his knees, shoulders heaving. Gasping for breath, he half turned to point behind him. The words wouldn't come. He dragged himself on his knees to the wooden water bucket and drank thirstily from the dipper.

"I saw them, Josh!" The words were still difficult to get out.

Thomas kept squinting into the distance. "I don't see anything, Muley. Maybe it was just deer, or some wild horses."

Muley shook his head violently. "No, sir! They were there, a whole bunch of them. On horseback."

Anxiously I asked, "Did they shoot at you, Muley?"

"No, Josh. They just sat there and looked at me. They didn't move. Didn't even say howdy." He paused. "I didn't say howdy, neither. I just lit out a-runnin'."

Thomas moved toward his rifle now. "It was likely his imagination, but we better go see."

I slung powder horn and shot pouch over my shoulder and saddled my horse. Muley and Thomas did the same, Muley still trembling from his scare. He pointed the way for us to go, but he was careful not to ride out in front. We skirted the newly-broken field and moved through scattered oak trees. We keep clear of underbrush where a red man might hide, though we scouted it for tracks. For a time Muley was positive where he had seen the Indians. But after a while he began to fidget uncertainly. I knew the signs well enough: Muley was lost.

Thomas had doubted from the first, and now I began doubting too. Muley sensed it, for he started pleading: "They was there, Josh. They was as real as you and me and that spotted dog. He barked at them. He wouldn't bark if they wasn't real, would he?"

I shook my head. "No Muley, he wouldn't." But the dog would bark at almost anything that moved. And it could have been anything.

We scouted and circled and saw nothing. At length Thomas pulled up. "We're wastin' our time, Josh."

Muley kept pleading, but I agreed with Thomas. "Sure, Muley," I said, trying to pacify him. "You saw them, but they've gone now."

We started back. I kept my gaze on the ground, looking for tracks. I didn't expect to see them. But suddenly, there they were. "Thomas, here's Muley's tracks when he was runnin' for home. You can see for yourself, he was travelin' pretty fast."

Thomas nodded. I said, "Let's backtrack them a ways. Can't hurt nothin' to do that. We can spare a little time."

Thomas didn't want to, but he gave in. "Let's hurry. We need to be gettin' that cabin up."

Taking the lead, I followed the sign of Muley's headlong rush. Presently Muley shouted, "Yonder's the place, Josh! Yonder's where I seen them at!"

A chill ran down my back, and for some reason the doubt left me. My grip tightened on the rifle. "Hang back a little, Thomas. Keep me covered."

I touched my heels to the horse's ribs and started ahead, nerves tightening.

Muley shouted. "That tree yonder, Josh. That's where they was."

Slowly I rode to a huge old live oak. I found the sign there, plain and fresh. There *had* been horses here—two of them. I called for Thomas and Muley to come up. Thomas studied the sign. "Wild horses, maybe."

I shook my head. "Not wild horses. I can feel it, Thomas."

Thomas nodded, after a moment. "So can I. It was Indians."

I pointed out, "They didn't shoot at Muley. Maybe they were friendly."

Thomas said grimly. "There were friendly Indians in Tennessee too, in Papa's time. But there was a heap of unfriendly ones. You couldn't hardly tell them apart till it was too late. Got so folks quit takin' any chances. The dead ones you could trust."

I glanced back at Muley. "Thomas, you're always too hard on Muley. You'll have to admit, he was right about this."

Thomas shook his head. "You don't have to have any sense to see Indians."

I fingered the rifle a long time. My hands had trembled awhile, but now they were steady again. The excitement had gone. "Well, we oughtn't to be surprised none. Folks told us there would likely be Indians. We won't leave here just because they showed up."

Thomas frowned. "No, Josh. Indians go with new land and westering, just like snakebite and the fever. We come to stay!"

Chapter Seven

After that we built the corral fence a little higher, and we rushed our construction work. To clear the view and help reduce the chance of surprise attack, we cut down most of the trees that stood near the rising cabin. When we weren't using the horses in the daytime, we staked them on fresh grass at the end of a long rope. At night we never failed to bring them into the corral and tie the gate shut with rawhide.

Several nights the spotted dog's barking woke us up, afraid Indian horse thieves were trying to open the corral. But always it turned out to be no more than a skunk or a coon, or at most a grazing deer.

One night the dog did not bark at all. Next morning Thomas went out to milk the cows and found fresh moccasin tracks near the corral.

Why the Indians hadn't taken the horses, we didn't know. "If they come stealin'," he said, frowning at Muley, "the first thing they'll take will be the watchdog. That hound of yours is cowardly and no-account."

Muley threw his arms protectively around the dog's neck. "He's a good dog. Sure enough, he is. You ain't fixin' to do somethin' to him, are you?"

Thomas left it to me to reassure Muley. "No, don't fret over that. But someday when we get time to visit the neighbors' we'll see if we can't get him some company. We need a dog around here we can depend on."

The time finally came when the cabin was up, the chimney finished, logs rived for clapboard shingles and the roof covered over so that it wouldn't leak badly in the rain. They always leaked a little, those days. The field had been hoed and the garden work caught up with. The corn was coming along nicely.

"Thomas," I said, "don't you think we ought to go now and get acquainted with the neighbors we haven't met yet? When the crops start to ripenin', we'll be busy again."

Thomas replied. "We've got along pretty good so far without worryin' about neighbors."

"But we might need them someday, and maybe they'll need us. We ought to get acquainted."

We had met the neighbors on the colony side as we came up here, unless of course some more had come in behind us. According to the map we had copied from Pounce's, the nearest neighbors upriver bore the name of Hernandez. I could tell that wasn't Irish.

Thomas grumbled, "I'd as soon not have any truck with Mexicans. I don't see how any good could come of it."

"They're there," I argued. "I don't expect they'll move away just because we've come. And like Jared said, we'll need all the friends we can get." The truth was, I was curious.

"Chances are we couldn't understand them noway. We'd have to make sign talk, like a bunch of Indians."

"Our rifles speak the same language. Mexicans or not, we'd want them with us if we ever have Indian trouble."

That kind of talk reached Thomas when nothing else would.

"We'll go," he said reluctantly.

We took Muley along, afraid to leave him by himself. We also took the extra horse, leading him for a pack animal. It wasn't so much that he was actually needed, but it didn't seem wise to leave him at home unattended if somebody with feathers in his hair should drop by to call. Anyway, before we reached the Hernandez place we might shoot a deer or two, as a courtesy. The extra horse would be handy to pack in the meat.

We found the country west of us to be much the same as our own—rolling hills with scattered oak and other timber, wide valleys with the grass so tall the seedheads brushed the soles of our shoes as we rode through it on horseback. The grass was still green at the base but maturing now in the summer sun. It was not as lush as in Tennessee, but the look and feel of it showed it was strong.

The cattle along the way confirmed that. They were in good flesh. These were wild-natured cattle of every color in the rainbow, with long horns and long legs that carried them with almost the swiftness of deer.

"Notice somethin' about these cattle, Thomas? They every one got a fire-brand on their hip. And it's always the same brand. Short of an H, done up stylish. H for Hernandez, I reckon."

Thomas was not impressed. "This far out, what difference would it make who they belonged to?"

"I'll bet they can drive these cattle down to the settlements and sell them for beef."

Interest sparked in Thomas's eyes. "You may have an idea, Josh. I'd put up my horse against Muley's spotted dog that these are plain wild cattle that was runnin' free. These Mexicans just gathered them and put their brand on them and made them their. We could do that too."

"Take them away from the Mexicans?"

"No, I don't mean that. But we could hunt down wild cattle and burn our brand on them and bring them down to our place. With our three cows and a bull, it's goin' to take us a long time to get a herd together. This way, we could rush things a right smart."

One of our cows had dropped a calf just after we had gotten here. Another had calved just a couple of days back. Thomas was right. Nature's way would be slow.

I said, "Maybe the Mexicans will teach us how they do it."

Thomas shook his head. "We can learn by ourselves."

I nodded, but the thought ran through my mind that I was going to ask anyway, if these Mexicans were friendly, and if we could find some way to talk to them.

Muley and I fell to talking. That is, Muley talked and I listened, about the deer and the wild turkeys and a coon that had gotten into the cabin. Gradually we dropped back somewhat behind Thomas. He rode up over a rise and pulled his horse to a sudden stop. He motioned excitedly for us to stay back. Slowly, carefully, Thomas slipped off of his horse. He motioned again for us to stay back, but I wouldn't have done it for a sackful of silver. I dismounted and moved up, leading my horse. Muley's eyes were wide with wonder as he came along behind me.

"What is it, Thomas?" Muley called innocently.

If Thomas could have found a quiet way to kill him, he might have done it then and there. He put his finger to his lips, then drew it slowly and pointedly across his throat. He turned angrily on me. "Why didn't you do what I told you?"

"Because I want to see."

What I saw made the hair bristle around my collar. Down in a flat, two men rode along horseback, side by side, rifles in their hands, ready to fire in an instant. Flanking them rode six Indians, three on each side. Two of the Indians carried lances. One had a gun of some sort. The other three held bows, with arrows strung and ready to loose. They moved in silent, patient menace.

"Cat and mouse," said Thomas. "They know they got those men in a trap, so now they're playin' it like a game."

"Six against two." A chill ran through me. "They could finish it in a second."

"They're wonderin' a little, though. Those two fellers have each got one shot to fire. When they die, they'll likely take a couple of Indians with them. That's what's holdin' the redskins off." He said it with calm detachment, as if what we watched were nothing more than a good checker game.

"Thomas, there's three of us. That would narrow the odds."

"It would if those were white men. But they're just a couple of Mexicans."

"That doesn't make any difference."

"It does to me. When my time comes to die, I want it to be for somethin' important. I say let the Mexicans take care of their own."

I put my foot into the stirrup. "Then you just sit here!"

Thomas caught my arm. "You're not goin' down there. It's not our put-in."

Muley's face paled. "Josh, don't you go and leave me."

I said, "You stay with Thomas."

Muley protested, "I want to stay with you, Josh."

Thomas didn't often swear, but he swore now at me. "You're as simple-minded as Muley is. But if you're bound and determined, I won't let you go by yourself and get killed." He swung onto his horse, his face twisted. "Just remember if these Mexicans slit our throats someday, this was your idea."

We put Muley in the middle, where he might be less of a hazard to himself and to us. Then, riding abreast, we walked our horses over the crest and started down the other side.

One of the lance-carrying Indians spotted us before we got down to the flat. He shouted and waved the lance. The Indians halted. The two Mexicans immediately turned their horses so that the men were back to back, facing out and ready to fire instantly in any direction. An Indian loosed an arrow. It missed us by a long way. I held my breath as we kept riding, the rifles cradled in our arms. I could see Muley's face whitening.

"Don't show them you're scared, Muley."

"I *am* scared."

"So am I, but we don't want them to know it."

"I'll try to grin at them, Josh."

The Indians stood their ground but loosed no more arrows at us. Thirty feet from them, Thomas said, "We better stop here."

We stopped, our rifles pointed at the Indians.

For a minute or two it was a contest of wills. They tried to stare us down. We stared back. At last one of the Indians spoke in a sharp voice. The six pulled their horses around and started away in a long trot.

One of the Mexicans shouted something I couldn't understand. They quickly stepped down from their saddles. "Down!" Thomas barked. Fifty yards away the Indians suddenly stopped and whirled around. The one who had a gun fired it. The ball fell short. The others loosed their arrows. One of the Mexican horses fell kicking and screaming.

Again the Indians wheeled and moved into a lope, away from us.

The horse threshed, an arrow in its flank. The Mexican waited until the horse laid its head upon the ground, then lowered his rifle and fired point blank. He turned gravely toward us and removed his big-brimmed hat. *"Grácias, señores."*

Thomas made no reply, so I did it. "Mister, I don't know what you're sayin', and I'm sorry about that."

The Mexican was in his early twenties, his face a light brown, his eyes black. The other was much younger, about sixteen. Their resemblance indicated that they were brothers. The older one made a weak attempt at a smile and gave it up. He was beginning to tremble now, the after-shock starting to reach him. "Too much excitement. I forgot, you do not understand."

I glanced at Thomas. "He speaks American."

The Mexican shook my hand, and I could feel the cold sweat on his palm. "I am called Ramón Hernandez. I speak a little, only, of the English."

"I'm Josh Buckalew, and I don't speak Mexican atall. That yonder is my brother Thomas. The other feller is Muley Dodd."

Muley shook hands. Thomas only nodded, staying where he was, aloof and vaguely disapproving. Hernandez turned to his brother. "And this is Felix."

Felix was quivering. The full weight of the experience had come crashing down on him. He settled to the ground and knelt with his shoulders shaking uncontrollably. He crossed himself. The older brother moved up beside him and spoke to him in a gentle voice.

"For Felix," he said apologetically, "this is the first time death is come so close. He can smell its breath."

I remembered how I had felt that night we fought the outlaws near Natchitoches. I could sympathize.

The Indians had disappeared. "You have much trouble with them?" I asked.

Ramón Hernandez shook his head. "Not many times. Most time they just want to steal horses. Today these young Indians, they find two Mexicans and think *Ay*, why not get two scalps to take home, show women. Very easy, he thinks. Comanche, he does not fight much when he is not sure he wins. You come, he goes."

"They might come back."

Ramón shrugged. "Maybe not for months again." He watched his brother as the boy regained his composure. "Where you come from?" he asked me.

I said, "We're neighbors. We got land, yonderways."

Ramón nodded, pleased. "Good to have people here. When some day we have enough people, Indians come no more."

He helped Felix to his feet. Felix gave us a shy, half-ashamed grin. He said something we didn't understand, and Ramón told us he was apologizing for acting like a woman. It would never happen again, he promised.

Ramón said, "Felix and me, we take you home with us. We want family to see you."

I could tell Thomas didn't like it, but I said, "We'd be right tickled."

Ramón smiled. "We will be friends. Maybe you teach me better the English.

I said, "Ain't no doubt about that. Time I get through ateachin' you, there won't be no college professor that talks better. Now, whichaway's the house?"

The Hernandez house blended into the land, and I didn't even see it at first. It was long and squat, almost flat-roofed, its walls of rock and its roof held up by timbers dragged from the banks of a creek nearby. Smaller houses and sheds clustered around the main house, all within easy running distance in case of attack. We rode through a scattering of cattle and passed a band of small native horses and little Mexican mules, these loose-herded on grass by a boy of ten or so. Half a dozen milk goats followed along, eyeing us with curiosity.

In a flat stretch of open ground beyond the house, a man and a boy with wooden plows and a mule apiece worked a field where young corn was up to a good stand. Nearer the house, women and small girls hoed a garden. They all stopped work to stare at us.

Ramón pointed toward an opening in the heavy corral, which was built of live-oak limbs stacked and wedged between pairs of stout posts. We rode in. A pair of boys came running at Ramón's call. He spoke to them in a fast-clipped Spanish that I could only marvel over. That language. I thought, was going to be a booger to learn.

We followed Ramón's lead and unsaddled. As we started toward the house, Felix and Muley somehow seemed to fall in with each other. Thomas followed along behind, making it plain he was not keen on any part of this.

Near the front door were two homemade crates, each containing a game rooster. The Mexican people all loved a cockfight.

"Mamá," Ramón called. *"Tenemos huéspedes."*

An elderly woman appeared in the open door of the long rock house, her brown hand up over her eyes. She peered out beyond the broad brush arbor that served in lieu of a porch. She greeted us cordially, even before Ramón began to tell her what had happened. I heard her gasp the word. *"Indios,"* and knew it meant Indians.

She came first to me, then to Muley, and finally to the flustered Thomas, kissing each of us in turn.

Hat off, I had to crouch a little to follow her into the house. Mexicans were inclined toward smallness, and so were their houses. Ramón pointed to several hand-made wooden chairs that had rawhide seats. "Please, it is not much. But sit. Be to home. This house is your house." When we were seated he said, "*Mamá* will bring you to drink. I bring the family."

As the gray-haired mother bustled about excitedly, I took a long look at the room. The house was stoutly built but Spartanly furnished. Almost everything appeared hand-built, probably right here. The rock walls were mostly bare, except for a few clothes pegs and a crude carved crucifix prominently displayed. Heavy shutters were hung inside each windowsill, with a bar which could be dropped to secure them. In each shutter was a small leather-hinged porthole, rifle-size.

"This is more than just a house. Thomas. This is a fort."

Thomas shook his head. "It don't look like much to me." Señora Hernandez brought black coffee. Coffee was very scarce out here. I knew she was cutting into a long-saved supply for us.

Ramón came back, trailed by half a dozen youngsters. "I want you to meet my brothers and sisters." He lined them up by ages, ranging from a boy of six or seven up to a pretty, black-eyed girl I guessed to be fourteen, or maybe fifteen. She was still lank and a little awkward, but in a year or two the woman would begin showing through. *Then* there would be visitors a-plenty to the Hernandez' door.

Ramón counted them off. "Here we have Enrique, Consuelo, José, Margarita, Alfredo and María." He looked back over his shoulder. "Teresa! *Dónde-estás*, Teresa?"

My heart leaped as a girl walked in. Girl? She was a

woman, the most beautiful woman I had ever seen.

Ramón said proudly, "Teresa is the oldest of the sisters."

Teresa bowed. I started to put out my hand but didn't know whether I was supposed to shake hands with her or not. I pulled it back, the color rising in my face. "Howdy, Miss Teresa."

Her answer was in Spanish. Disappointment touched me, for we wouldn't be able to talk to each other. Not, at least, until I learned Spanish. And suddenly I knew I was going to learn in a hurry.

A shadow fell across the open doorway. Another brother stood there, one I judged to be nearly as old as Ramón. He scowled, his gaze touching first Thomas, then Muley, then me. He said something in a sharp voice.

Ramón's smile dimmed, but he managed to hold part of it. He said, "This is my brother Antonio. Next to me, he is the oldest. Next to me, he runs the family since our father is gone. *Next to me*." He said something sharp to Antonio, and Antonio quit scowling.

Ramón retold for the brothers and sisters what had happened to him and Felix. I found Teresa watching me, and my gaze dropped away from her. It was the younger girl, María, who stepped forward and stood almost toe-to-toe with me. She spoke words I could not understand, but I could read the gratitude in her eyes.

Ramón explained. "María, she says she wish to speak English, so she can say to you how much thanks she has in her heart."

I said. "Tell her, Ramón, that I'll come over here as often as I can. I'll teach her to talk American." I glanced shyly toward Teresa. "I'll teach all of those who want to learn."

Ramón translated. María clapped her hands. I found

Teresa smiling. This time I kept my nerve and returned the smile.

Antonio did not miss the look that passed between Teresa and me, he spoke in anger. Ramón answered him in words that cut like a whip. Antonio's eyes pierced me with hostility. He pointed first at me, then at Teresa, and said something more. Then he turned on his heel and strode out of the house.

I saw Teresa drop her gaze, hurt.

"What was that all about?" I asked.

Ramón's face was darker than it had been. "Antonio has a strong mind. He does not like Americans."

Thomas spoke for the first time, belligerently. "What's wrong with Americans?"

Ramón shrugged. "For me, nothing. I have *Americano* friends. They teach me this little English I speak. I learn much from them, and I hope teach them a little. But Antonio is like some others of my people—he hates those who are not the same as he is."

I offered, "Maybe some American did him dirty."

Ramón shook his head. "No, but he thinks they will, someday. So he hates *now*."

Thomas snorted. "That's a hell of a thing, hatin' us for no cause."

The thought ran through my mind that Antonio was no different in that respect than Thomas. My brother must have read the thought in my eyes. "It's not the same thing," he said defensively.

"Ain't it?"

I glanced again at Teresa and found she had turned her face away. "Ramón," I said, "Antonio said somethin' about Teresa and me."

"It is not important."

"He must have thought so."

Ramón shrugged. "He says I should tell you Teresa

is—how you say?—promised. She has a man who will be her husband."

That came like a dash of cold water in my face. But I tried to keep it from showing.

Ramón said, "Many years ago it is decided, by our father and by the father of Diego Esquivel."

My mouth dropped open. "They decided? Didn't she have any say-so?"

"She was only a child. This is a matter for the fathers."

"It don't hardly seem fair to her . . ."

"Diego is a good man. Good friend of mine."

"Does she love him?"

Ramón shrugged again. "One learns to love, as one learns to speak English, or Spanish. It is the way of our fathers."

Thomas muttered, "I don't see why it should make any difference to you, Josh."

But I looked into the beautiful eyes of Teresa Hernandez, and I knew it was going to matter to me. It was going to matter a lot.

Chapter Eight

The people kept coming, some with proper papers and some without. Legal or contraband, they trekked across Texas in a hungry search for a fresh start, for land of their own. It was a restless time, a reaching time. Men prowled and hunted until they found what they liked, and then they planted their boots there and claimed it. Sometimes Mexican soldiers came and moved them on, but more often no one came, no one challenged, for the land was still broad and open, and there was room for so many more. What did it matter to a man what was written on paper five hundred miles away when he could reach down right here and scoop up a handful of black earth and almost feel the life throbbing in it? Who cared whether government spoke Spanish or English when the sky was big and blue and the land called out to a man in a voice that touched the soul?

They were all kinds, these early Texians. Most of them

came to farm and raise their families and mind their own business. They came seeking peace and opportunity, not a fight.

But there were some who seemed to be looking for trouble from the time they dropped their saddles to the grass and claimed their ground. Four miles to the south of us, three men made camp and started clearing the land. Two were young brothers. Jacob and Ezekiel Phipps, late of Kentucky. They had come to Texas for the same reasons we had—their father had sent them in search of a virgin land, just as he himself had searched a generation before. They were a decent pair—loud but basically honest—with one bad weakness: they were easily led.

And leading them was a shouting, cursing, irascible old reprobate named Alfred Noonan. Stocky, red-faced, he had been in Texas several times, off and on, through the last ten years. He told us something he evidently had not chosen to tell any of the authorities who granted him his land: once he had smuggled forbidden trade goods down into Mexico. During this enterprise he had been hounded and hunted and shot at by Mexican soldiers, so he nursed a virulent hatred of Mexicans in general and officials in particular. He had managed to rub off this feeling onto the Phipps brothers, though neither of them had ever seen enough Mexicans to count on their fingers—if, in fact, they could count at all.

Thomas, of course, had already developed a strong dislike for Mexicans. So he fell in with Noonan and the Phipps brothers like a thirsty duck that has found a water hole.

We all went down to help them raise their cabin. By the time that job was done I'd had enough of Noonan to last me for twenty years. I never went back. But Thomas went often, and sometimes they came to our cabin.

I could always predict what Noonan would say. "She's too good of a country to be run by a bunch of ignorant Mexicans. I say the United States ought to wade in here with an army and just naturally take over the whole shebang."

When Thomas and Noonan got started talking, it was always a marathon of sedition, with the Phipps brothers eagerly joining in like a pair of young coon dogs following the older hounds. Seemed Noonan always knew of a revolution brewing somewhere down in Mexico—there had been a lot of them—and he was full of ideas about how he and Thomas and the Phipps boys could smuggle guns in there and get rich.

I tried to tell Thomas he ought to steer clear of the old man. Thomas would simply shake his head. "It's all just talk—you ought to be able to tell that. Ain't none of it ever goin' to come to pass."

"This is dangerous talk. You know what Colonel Austin said about us gettin' mixed up in Mexican politics."

"I'd rather be mixed up in their politics than mixed up in their families. The kind of friends *you* got, you have no call to be talkin' about mine."

The argument always came down to that, sooner or later. I'd been going over to the Hernandez *rancho* often. I always tried to explain to Thomas that I was only going so I could learn to talk Mexican, and to teach the Hernandez family how to speak American. But Thomas figured all along that my main interest was in Teresa Hernandez.

And he was right.

María, fifteen, was the best learner. She picked up English faster than any of the others excepting Ramón, of course, who already had a fair knowledge of it. María showed so much interest in learning that Ramón helped her when I wasn't there. That way, she had a long head start on the others.

Teresa was learning English, too. But English was only her secondary interest in the lessons, as Spanish was mine.

Muley always went with me. He never did really get the hang of Spanish; his mind just wasn't bent toward learning. Yet, it always amazed me how he got along with the smaller members of the Hernandez family. They communicated through act and expression, rather than through the words they said. In the years since, I've seen Mexican and American kids get along like cousins without either really knowing a word the other spoke. There's an understanding between children that has nothing to do with words. And Muley, in many ways, was a child. He always would be.

Language wasn't important to Teresa and me, either. We understood each other without stumbling over the problems of translation. A glance, a quick touching of the fingertips when nobody was looking . . . we didn't really need to talk.

The trouble was, though, that we were never alone. Always, someone managed to be nearby, letting us know we were watched. Often it was her mother, sometimes one of the brothers or sisters. Occasionally it was the smoldering Antonio, hating me because my eyes were blue and my skin was light, making it plain that he never intended either of us to forget Teresa was already promised.

Neither did Thomas. He pointed it out every time I started toward the Hernandez place, and he would repeat it when I got back.

Back in Tennessee I had usually taken whatever advice appealed to me, and let the rest alone. I didn't change my ways much in Texas. I let Thomas advise me about planting and plowing and such, but when it came to Teresa I just didn't figure he knew much.

Through the long summer I kept going, and I kept learning. I got so I understood Spanish tolerably well.

I learned more than language. Ramón and Felix taught me a lot about their way of handling the wild native cattle. They taught me the fundamentals of using the rawhide *reata* to catch animals, and I practiced it until I was a fair-to-middling hand. I learned how the Mexicans captured wild cattle and took the vinegar out of them, fire-branding them with a hot iron that stamped a permanent claim of ownership on them.

The Hernandez brothers hated working in the fields and did as little of it as they could get by with. They enjoyed breaking wild horses to ride, or gathering wild cattle and putting their brand on them. That was hard work, but it had an excitement to it that a man never found behind a plow.

Even there, I found there were basic differences between my outlook and that of Ramón Hernandez. Sometimes it would be only the middle of the afternoon and there would still be plenty of cattle nearby for the taking. But he would hold up his hand and say:

"Enough. It has been a good day. One does not want to be greedy."

"Ramón," I would argue, "it's a long time till dark. Why quit now?" Usually I would talk to him in English and he would answer me in Spanish, for that way each of us would express himself best and still be understood.

"Work was made for the convenience of man, and not man for the work. Besides, over that hill lies the home of the most beautiful Gloria Vesquez, and I would like to go and pay my respects. After all, she might one day be the mother of my sons."

Other times it might be Catarina Torres, or Silvia

Martinez y Flores, or Margarita Sanchez. No matter. He was always watching for the woman who would be his wife. He said he did not know yet what she looked like, but he thought he would know her when she crossed his path.

Felix would smile and shrug as if to say he and I might as well go home.

Thomas never would admit that anything good came from my being around the Mexicans. But he was quick to pick up the use of the *reata* and the cattle-handling skill I had learned from the Hernandez men—Ramón, Felix and Antonio. Yes, even Antonio. For, to give the devil his due, I guess Antonio was the best cowman of them all, and horseman too. If he hated hard, he also worked hard . . . harder than Ramón.

It was as if his hatred gave him a special drive. Thomas had that drive too. It crossed my mind often that Thomas and Antonio had a lot in common, but of course they would not ever stop and compare.

In time, Thomas and Muley and I had a fair-sized bunch of cattle with our own brand on them, cattle whose ancestors had strayed from the pastures of the Spanish missions and had gone the way of the wild herds. Come fall, we would pick out the fattest and drive them down to the settlements to trade for supplies, and maybe even a little coin.

I mentioned Felix. He was a year older than María, just at the age when he was looking for somebody to follow. One time it would be the grinning Ramón. Another, it would be the brooding Antonio, who had a way of making a sunny day dark. If Felix was dark and morose, he was following Antonio. If he was joking and enjoying himself, it was Ramón day.

A constant rivalry existed between the older brothers, each trying to bring Felix into his own camp to stay. I sensed that there probably had been a rivalry of one kind or another between Ramón and Antonio from the time Antonio had first grown big enough to hurl a rock in anger.

It pleased me to see that Felix followed Ramón more than he followed Antonio. Felix had the makings of a good man, if he didn't choose wrong.

From what Ramón told me about Diego Esquivel, the man Teresa was pledged to marry, he sounded all right. Under different circumstances I wouldn't have hated him. But I lay awake nights, tortured by the thought of his taking Teresa in forced marriage, closing the door behind them and shutting her out of my life. It didn't help much that Ramón said Diego was none too ready for marriage himself. Esquivel was enjoying all the pleasures and privileges of bachelorhood and, among the gay young maidens of Bexar, these were considerable. He had seen Teresa but few times in recent years and had no more romantic interest in her than he might have had in any pretty girl.

Yet I knew that her beauty would quickly develop that interest, once she was his wife. Worse—she might even learn to enjoy his love, eventually. He would have what I had not even dared hope for. Though the sight of Teresa fired my blood, I had had nothing more from her than her smiles and fleeting touches of her hand. Not once had I ever been able to kiss her.

Except for Antonio Hernandez, I might have had a chance. The rest of the family liked me. There was, of course, the old family tradition of the arranged marriage. Even this we might have worked out in some honorable way, had I been allowed the opportunity to reason with Diego Esquivel.

Always there was Antonio and that implacable hatred,

standing like a barred door between Teresa and me. I should have expected the thing he did, but it came as a surprise.

One day when Muley and I rode in to the Hernandez place, we found the family strangely silent. María, who usually met me at the door, smiling, only glanced in sadness, then turned away. Teresa was in the front room. I saw tears as her eyes met mine.

"Teresa, what's wrong?"

She ran, crying.

Ramón took my arm. "Josh . . . friend . . . let us go out into the cool of the arbor. We have something to talk about."

I sent Muley to play with the kids, because that was why he came.

Ramón was grave. "First of all, let us be honest. For a long time we have known of your feeling for Teresa. And we have known she felt strongly about you. But you were told from the first that she was promised, in the manner of our people. Perhaps we should have done something to stop this at the beginning, when there would have been little pain. But you were our friend, and we did not know how. Now there is no choice. The pain has to come.

"Do not ask me why Antonio hates you. Do not even ask him, for he does not know, except that you are of one people and we are of another. He has not liked what has happened between you and Teresa. He has taken it upon himself to stop it. He went to Bexar. He talked with Diego Esquivel, and together they planned the wedding. Diego is on his way here now, with his family and the priest. The wedding will be tomorrow."

It was as if he had slashed me with a knife.

"Ramón, she doesn't love him. She doesn't even know him."

Ramón shrugged. "What can be done? It is the tradition. Love comes, and love goes. But tradition lasts forever."

"To hell with tradition. I love her, and she loves me!"

"She will learn to love Diego. It is our people's way."

"I'll take her away from here. I'll make her one of *my* people."

Ramón shook his head. "You cannot do that. She has too much honor to go against the wishes of her father, rest his soul."

I pushed to my feet and strode into the house, Ramón following. I found Mrs. Hernandez in the front room with Teresa and Antonio, watching me worriedly. I spoke in the best Spanish I knew.

"Teresa, this is not going to happen. I'm not going to allow it. You're going to marry *me*!"

Her mother stood silent, shocked beyond speaking. But Antonio's voice lashed at me. "Away from here, American! Teresa is not yours, and she will never be yours! She stays among her own."

I grabbed Teresa's hand. "Come on, I'm taking you away."

I didn't even see the knife until Teresa screamed. There was a blur of a hand, the flash of the blade. He held the point against my throat. It burned like fire. Antonio's voice was as sharp as the steel. "I would see both of you dead first. Turn loose her hand, American, or you die right now!"

His black eyes seethed. He meant exactly what he said. Teresa jerked her hand away and screamed, "Antonio, no!"

Ramón stopped it. "Put the knife away, Antonio!" His voice was quiet, but it carried an authority that penetrated even the fury of Antonio Hernandez. Antonio lowered the knife. I could see a small spot of red on the point, and I could feel a burning where he had brought the blood.

Ramón turned to me. "Josh, we have enjoyed your company here many times. We had hoped nothing would ever come between us to spoil it. But now we must ask you to leave. We must keep the door shut against you until the wedding is over and Teresa is gone. Please go now, and go quietly."

That was it, courteous but to the point. The Mexican people had a courtly way of telling you to go to hell.

There seemed little choice at the moment. I would have to hurt some one—maybe even kill—to get Teresa out of here now. I backed toward the door.

"Wait for me, Teresa. I'll come for you."

Antonio gritted, "Come back and you will be buried here!"

Ramón said, "Please go, Josh. Lose gracefully, so we may still be friends."

I said, "I haven't lost yet."

All the way home I tried to decide what I was going to do. I couldn't develop any definite plan. All I knew was that after dark I was going back, and somehow I was going to break Teresa out of there. Maybe I could get Thomas to help me. And if he wouldn't, I had friends downriver who would.

It was nearly dark when Muley and I reached the cabin. Thomas had the cow milked and the horses penned. I saw three extra horses in the corral.

Muley saw them too. "The Phipps boys are here. And that old man Noonan. He sure does talk a right smart, don't he, Josh? Half the time I don't know what he's talkin' about."

"Neither does he."

The dog set in to barking and brought Thomas to the

door, rifle in his hand. It was always like that with Muley's dog: bark when there wasn't any need for it, and hide when he should be making a racket. Thomas said, "Wasn't lookin' for you back. Thought you'd spend the night with them Mexicans again."

I could tell by the sound of his voice that he and Noonan had been talking, and he was in a mood to argue with me about the Hernandez family. I was in no temper for it.

"Thomas, I got to talk to you, and I got to do it right now." I saw the visitors come to the door, their curiosity aroused. "Out in the corral. By ourselves."

Thomas glanced at his company and said he'd be back directly. He followed Muley and me to the corral. I unsaddled and waited until Muley had done the same. "Go on to the house, Muley."

He protested. "I don't want to have to listen to old man Noonan."

"Go listen to him anyway."

Muley grumbled and walked off. I told Thomas that Diego Esquivel was on his way to marry Teresa. Thomas nodded in satisfaction. "Well, maybe now you can set your mind on your plowin'."

"But he's not goin' to marry her. I am."

"How you figure that? I don't expect them Mexicans are goin' to throw roses in your path and tell you to come take her."

"I'm takin' fresh horses, and I'm goin' back to get her tonight. I'm goin' to break her out of there. I want you to help me, Thomas."

"Me? Are you crazy?"

"You're my brother, Thomas. I've never asked you for much. I know you don't agree with me about Teresa, but I hope you'll be a big enough man to put that aside now and help me."

A deep frown creased his face. "Josh, goin' over there and lovin' her up is one thing. Actually marryin' her is somethin' else."

"I'm goin' to do it, with your help or without it. I just hoped it would be with your help."

Thomas stared at me a long moment, then turned away. I didn't realize what he was going to do until he opened the gate. Then he turned and waved his hat, shouting at the horses.

Before I could move, they were on their way out of the corral.

"Damn you, Thomas!"

I ran to my saddle and grabbed a rawhide *reata*. I yelled. "Muley, come help me."

Thomas stood in the gate. As I started around him, his fist came at me. It slammed me back against the fence. Thomas called for his friends, and they came running. The four of them moved in on me. I tried to lunge at Thomas, but strong hands grabbed and held me. Thomas's fist drove into my stomach. All my breath left me.

"Now, Josh," Thomas gritted, "just quit it. What we're doin' we're doin' for your own good."

I heard Muley yelp and saw him come running to help me. I tried to yell at him to stay where he was, but no sound would come. He plowed in with fists swinging. One of the Phipps boys backhanded him, then slashed at him with a rock-like set of knuckles that bent Muley back like a small boy. He dropped.

Thomas told them what was happening. "Looks like we'll just have to tie Josh up and keep him awhile. Never thought I'd see the day I'd have to do this to my own flesh and blood."

I struggled against them, but they had me so tight there wasn't a chance to break loose.

Noonan said, "Thomas, what do you say we take them

over to our cabin a spell? There's more of us to keep an eye on them there. And if drastic measures is called for, we might come nearer takin' them than you would, bein' his brother and all."

Thomas frowned. "I don't want him hurt none."

"We'll just kind of salt them down, both of them. You won't have to fret none or feel the least bit uneasy. Come tomorrow, Josh'll still be a happy bachelor. And you won't have no Mexican kinfolks."

My breath was coming back. "I'll get you! I'll get all of you!"

Noonan didn't seem impressed. "Sure you will, Josh. But for now you're goin' to come on along like a good boy. Thomas, how about you bringin' them horses back in?"

After a while the horses came. I tried to fight free, and Jacob Phipps fetched me a clout that put me on my knees. He pushed me down onto my stomach and sat on me while the others saddled up. Then he pulled me to my feet. "We'll be a-leavin' now, Josh. It's up to you whether you get on that horse by yourself or if we clout you again and put you up there."

I knew I didn't have the strength for a fight, so I climbed up. I had some notion of being able to pull loose from them down the trail and get away. I wanted to save my strength for that possibility. But I found they weren't going to give me the chance. They tied my hands to the saddle. Then they tied a short rope to the reins. Ezekiel Phipps held the end of the rope in his big hands.

Muley sobbed. "I tried. Josh. I did try."

"Sure, Muley. You did right good. There was just too many of them."

Thomas said, "Josh, don't you do nothin' to make them have to hurt you, do you hear? The time'll come when you'll thank me for this."

In my fury there was nothing I could say that was half enough. So I held my tongue. I'd be back, and there would be a reckoning.

They kept us tied all that night, and all the next day and night. They untied Muley to let him eat. They tried untying me once but tied me up again when I attempted to fight my way out of the cabin. If I had any satisfaction at all, it was that I had left my mark on all of them. The afternoon of the wedding, Noonan rode to the Hernandez place and spied on it from a distance. He came riding in next morning, satisfied.

"It was quite a sight, Josh. You ought to've seen it. When them Mexicans throw a celebration, they sure do it up right."

I knew without asking, but I had to ask anyway, the dread coming up in me heavy and cold. "They're married?"

"Sure enough. Handsome-lookin' couple, best I could tell. You got to understand I was too far away to see real clear. I doubt as she'll miss you much, Josh. Mexican gals have got a talent for lovin', and I expect that boy will keep her too busy to be frettin' herself about some calf-eyed *Americano*." He glanced at Jacob and Ezekiel. "Reckon you'd just as well untie him and let him go."

Jacob went to work on the knots that bound me. "Josh, I hope you'll take this in the spirit we meant it. We was just doin' you a favor."

When my hands were free, I rubbed my raw wrists to get the circulation going. I would need it for what I wanted to do.

Jacob grinned at me. "No hard feelin's, Josh."

I don't know where the strength came from, but my fist caught his nose dead-center. His head snapped back and cracked against the log siding. I whirled and caught

Ezekiel in the ribs. He grunted and doubled over.

Noonan hobbled toward the door, his eyes wide. "Now Josh, you wouldn't go and hurt an old man."

I stopped, for dizziness came over me. Noonan said. "You're sure an ungrateful kind. Josh. No wonder you're such a burden to your brother."

I reached for him but missed. He ran out of the cabin, shouting and cursing at me. I untied Muley. We walked out into the daylight. It hurt my eyes at first, but that was only a small addition to the agony I felt in body and in spirit. The whole world had fallen in on me.

I caught up our horses, trying to choke down the rage which fought for release. I think if I had had a gun I would have gone back into the cabin and killed all three men, or tried to.

"Muley, you ride on home."

"What you fixin' to do, Josh?"

"I'm goin' to the Hernandez place."

"Seems like it's a little late now, don't it? I mean, they said there had done been a weddin' and all that. There ain't nobody but God can undo a weddin', is there?"

"Just go on home, Muley."

"When you figure on bein' back?"

"I don't know. Just look for me when you see me comin'."

Eight days came and went before the night I finally rode up to our cabin. I swung down woodenly and unsaddled, turning the horse into the corral and tying the gate. Muley's dog barked at me. I trudged to the cabin, my head down, my throat in a knot.

Thomas opened the door and stood there against the candlelight, rifle in his hand. "Josh? That you, Josh?"

I walked in past him without being able to look into his face.

"Josh, it's been over a week. Where you been?"

I couldn't answer him at first.

He stared at me. "You're sure makin' it hard on yourself. You've been blinded by somethin' you take to be love. Hell, you don't even know what love is. You never felt it before, and the first time you get a real itch toward a woman you think you're in love with her. This'll all blow over, and you'll thank me. You'll look at her and tell me how glad you are that you're not tied to her."

Voice came to me. "I'll never see her again. Thomas, nobody will."

His mouth dropped open.

I said, "She's dead, Thomas."

I think that was the first time he ever really saw how deeply and honestly I had been in love with Teresa. "Dead? But how?"

"The mornin' after they were married, the two of them set out alone toward Bexar, ahead of the others. When the Esquivel family came along later they found them . . . what the Indians had left of them."

Thomas looked at the floor, his face frozen. "My God, Josh. . . ."

I said, "If I'd gone back that night, she'd still be alive. I'd have gotten her away from there, and I'd have taken her back toward the settlements, where there wouldn't have been any Indians. That's how it would have been, Thomas, if you hadn't stopped me."

"I was thinkin' of you, Josh."

"Or maybe you were just thinkin' of yourself, and how bad you'd hate to have a Mexican woman for your sister-in-law."

Thomas shook his head. "What can I say?"

"It'd be better if you didn't say anything."

He brought himself to look at me. "Josh, that was over a week ago. Where have you been all this time?"

"Been lookin' for some Indians to kill."

He stared. "Find any?"

I shook my head. "They disappeared like smoke."

"But a week, Josh. How come you to stay so long?"

"Afraid to come back any sooner. Afraid I might kill you." I could see the hurt in his eyes. "I won't do it, though. I got over that much of it. But from now on I'm through lettin' you think for me. I'm through listenin' to you. I don't even want to see you."

Thomas put his hand on my shoulder. "Josh . . ."

I couldn't hold it any longer. I hit him. And when I saw him stagger back, all the anger and all the grief that had banked up in me seemed to explode at once. I tied into him, slashing, jabbing.

It was years before I could think back on it without my emotions getting in the way. Long afterward, remembering, I knew Thomas didn't do much to defend himself. He took all I had to give him, and what I gave him would have killed a lesser man. I fought him until all the strength had ebbed out of me and I lay on the earthen floor of the cabin, sobbing like a little boy.

For a long time I lay there, letting the hurt have its way with me. But finally I pushed to my feet and saw Thomas sitting on a rawhide chair, regarding me gravely. His face was bruised and swollen, his clothing torn. But in his eyes was only sadness.

"Well, Thomas," I said, "which one of us is it goin' to be?"

"What do you mean?"

"I mean one of us has got to go. Will it be you, or me?"

Thomas's voice was hollow. "It's that bad, is it?"

"It's that bad."

He dug into his pocket. "I wish it wasn't this way,

Josh." He brought forth a coin. "This is gold. Come all the way with us from Tennessee. You call it."

"Heads I go, tails you do."

The coin caught the candlelight for an instant as it flipped out of Thomas's hand, went up, then fell. It made a faint thump on the floor. Thomas leaned over and picked it up. "Tails."

"I didn't see it," I said.

"That's what it was, though. Tails. The place is yours."

I nodded, too numb really to care which one of us went. "I want you to go tonight, Thomas!"

That shook him, but he shrugged. "All right."

He gathered up a few of his belongings, rolled his bedding and stepped out into the night to fetch his horse.

Muley said, "Josh, it's awful dark out there. It ain't good to turn a man out into the night thisaway."

"I'd have gone, if it had come up heads."

Muley said with an innocent wisdom that would come back to haunt me in the years ahead: "Maybe it did, Josh."

Chapter Nine

Hard work has never been popular, but it is a merciful healer.

Since Thomas had left, it was up to Muley and me to bring in the crops that fall. If I hadn't been up moving before daylight and laboring like a gray mule until dark, then flopping on my cot too tired to move, I might not have brought myself through those first dark weeks. Even with the work, I would glance up every so often and see Teresa's face in the autumn-red fringe of timber.

If it had been the beautiful face of those fleeting days we had together, I could have stood it. But always I saw her as I had seen her in death, the eyes and mouth open in horror, the blood dried to a sickening blackish crimson. The heart would drop out of me.

At such times, some men drown themselves in liquor. I had no liquor, so I tried to drown myself in work. There was more than enough of it. Muley suffered, because he tried with all that was in him to keep up with me. It's a wonder I didn't kill him.

Thomas stayed out of my sight. Muley tried to hide it from me, but in his guileless way he let me find out that Thomas would come around now and again, when I was somewhere else. Thomas would look things over, question Muley a little, then fade away before I got back. Much of the time he was staying with Noonan and the Phipps boys, helping them bring in wild cattle the way he and I had done, or helping them harvest their crops. At that time of year there was always work for a man like Thomas who wanted to hire out and didn't balk at hard labor. Usually he was paid in kind, for coin was scarce.

Once, I learned, Thomas went off on a long trip with Noonan somewhere to the south. Not for the world would I have admitted it, but I worried about him. I knew Noonan had him mixed up in a smuggling venture or something of that kind. Trouble and contention were like food and drink to Noonan's breed.

Muley got lonesome sometimes, with just the two of us there on the place. "When we goin' back to see the Hernandez family again?" he would ask.

"I don't know if I can ever go back," I told him. "Teresa's gone."

"The rest of them ain't gone. The kids are still there. I like them kids, Josh."

I could sympathize with Muley's loneliness, for I had my own. But I couldn't bring myself to visit again the place where I had known Teresa. Most of all, I knew I could not bear the sight of Antonio Hernandez. Always turning in my mind was the grim certainty that it had been his hatred—and Thomas's—which had killed her. Their blind, selfish, senseless hatred. . . .

The long months went by and Ramón came to see us

finally, he and Felix. Muley and I were working in the field where our small crop of cotton had matured into a blanket of white fluff. Ramón sat on his horse and watched me.

"You do not look good, friend Josh. You have carried grief badly."

I laid down my cotton sack. I felt resentment at first, for he could have called a halt to the wedding if he had not been so hide-bound to tradition. He could have spoken one word and stopped it.

"How is a man supposed to carry grief, Ramón? It's a heavy burden, no matter how you try to pick it up."

"Ours is the grief, too. We could help you carry it, if you would but ask."

I shook my head. "I'll tote my own load."

"We have not seen you in a long time."

I turned away and picked up my cotton sack. Ramón and Felix got off their horses. Muley ran forward to pump Felix's hand, his face shining with pleasure. Ramón fell in beside me and silently began to help, putting cotton into my sack. He had probably never picked any before, because the Mexicans themselves rarely grew it. Cotton had come in with the Americans. Sometimes I wondered why we tried it, living so far from the market: we couldn't eat it, and we didn't spin it, but we could trade it for coffee and flour and other necessities down in the settlements. The necessities were so hard to come by that they were almost considered luxuries. As for luxuries, there just weren't any.

Ramón and Felix soon had their fingers torn and sore from the hard, dry burs. Ramón said disapprovingly, "I had rather break my neck with the wild cattle and horses than to break my back in the cotton."

I had softened a little, working beside him. "There's not much fun in a cotton field," I admitted. "But cotton sells, and there's precious little else that does."

"What is money, that one must do so many unpleasant things to get it?"

"Why, Ramón, money is . . . Well, I mean, a man's just got to have money."

He shook his head. "Among our people there are some who live a lifetime and never feel a piece of silver cross their palm. A man can live from the land, if he will be content with what the land chooses to give him. This growing of cotton is not a natural thing, like hunting. Do you see the deer or the wolf or the buffalo planting cotton? No, they live as God intended them to, from what the land itself provides. If He had intended that we have cotton, He could have planted it Himself. This kind of work does no honor to a man."

"Work *is* honor. The Book says that by the sweat of the brow shalt thou earn thy bread."

"I had rather sweat my brow running the wild cattle. What could a man want that would make him do dishonoring work to get money? He cannot eat money. He cannot wear it. All he can do is trade it for something he wants. A few beans, a little corn, enough beef—what more could a man want?"

I knew Ramón was purposely working up an argument with me to take my mind away from Teresa. I also knew he was dead serious in what he said.

He went on, "In the Book you learn of the lilies of the field. They do not toil, neither do they spin. And of a certainty you find no lilies in a field of cotton."

I let go my cotton sack while I wiped the sweat from my brow. It gave me a righteous feeling to know I was earning my bread like the Book said to. But it never had occurred to me that there might be conflict between that part of the Word and the passage Ramón had quoted.

I said, "It's all in the way a man looks at it, I reckon.

You and me, we just naturally look at it different."

"I think, my friend, this is the big problem between your people and mine. There is little understanding. Perhaps there never will be. Your people say my people are lazy—that they work no more than they have to. My people say your people are greedy—that you work too long and too hard to get money for things you do not need and that you do not take time to taste life for the good flavor that is in it.

"In too many ways we are different. We shall never be alike."

Ramón was wise enough to see it, though it took me a long time to admit he was right. Even then, so long before the final and complete break came to Texas, the long shadows of the future were beginning to stretch out across the bold new land. No one ever really left the old country when he came to the new. Wherever the settler ventured, he took with him his customs and beliefs, the individual ways of the land he had come from. That applied to both American and Mexican. There was no such thing as a fresh, clean start. He resisted whatever was alien to the things he had known before.

True, the American and the Mexican found some points they could agree on. They might join to face the common enemy—the Indian. They could and did get together when it was to their advantage to trade. Individually, they made friends, as I had done with the Hernandez family. Some intermarried, as Jim Bowie had done in Bexar.

But basically, they remained two different kinds of people in outlook. There had been a time, in the beginning, when they might have stressed the points in which they were alike. Instead, they dwelt upon the differences. It is a human trait—not one of the better ones, but one which usually crops out. Where Mexicans and Americans lived in the same areas, the tendency was to group with their own kind. The dividing boundary might be a river or creek: it might be only an imaginary line. But real or imaginary, it was always there.

Often, in looking back, I have tried to decide for myself who was really to blame for it, who had started it. And always the answer comes up the same: nobody, and everybody. The tendency was there in the beginning, and it was on both sides.

That is the great irony of it all: the fact that we pulled apart and made so much of our difference only proved how much alike we were.

It was a big and open country, but bad news had a way of traveling fast. A foretaste of trouble came when a Texian force attacked the guardhouse at Anahuac, on the coast, to release prisoners who had been wrongfully taken. Excitement rippled through the colonies, and it left its mark even after the Mexican government moved to correct the situation that had brought on the trouble. Shortly afterward came a battle at Velasco, when a Mexican garrison tried to stop the sailing of a Texian ship that carried two cannon. The Mexicans ran out of ammunition, and the Texians persuaded them it would be wise to head south without undue delay.

I didn't see him, but I learned that Thomas had joined Noonan and the Phipps brothers for a fast ride to the coast as soon as they heard. By the time they got there, the smoke had cleared. Diplomatically-minded Texians and Mexicans were working to mend the breach that had been torn by their more warlike friends.

If the battles had any good result, it was that Mexico pulled most of her garrison out of Texas. They had been manned mostly by convict soldiers and others of poor repute. They had been a festering sore—a constant reminder that Mexico didn't really trust her new citizens from the north. Santa Ana was a revolutionary leader in Mexico in those days. He took the Texians' side after Anahuac and Velasco. A fresh wave of enthusiasm swept through the old settlers. Here, it seemed, was a new Mexican leader who understood and liked these blue-eyed foreigners—a Mexican who was going to give us all a fair deal.

There was a time—a short time—when it seemed we were about to get the world by the tail with a downhill pull. Mexico let up some on its immigration laws. More people crowded in. It got so that on an early fall morning when the air was crisp. I could hear a neighbor's ax ringing from across the hill.

But not all the newcomers were farmers and stockmen.

Once in a great while there was reason for Muley and me to go to San Felipe. It had grown, stretching out far along the Brazos. It was crowded with lawyers and land men, promoters of every kind. They worked little—some of them. But they never ceased talking, never stopped agitating. Wherever they found muddy water, they stirred it.

One spring day of 1833, Muley and I were nearing San Felipe in our wagon when we came across a familiar figure astride a bay horse. He rode toward us with head down, lost in his meditation. He didn't seem to see us until we were almost upon him.

Muley called, "Howdy, Colonel Austin."

Austin stopped and brought up his hand in greeting. He studied us, trying for recognition. "I'm sorry," he said. "I was absorbed with some worries of my own."

There had been plenty of them. His face was haggard, his eye bleak.

"I should know you," he said. "The faces are familiar."

"Joshua Buckalew, Colonel. And Muley Dodd. We live up yonder on the Colorado. You granted us the land."

He frowned. "Buckalew? Would you be the one who has been making so much talk of war?"

I shook my head and looked down. "I expect that'd be my brother, sir. His name is Thomas. Him and me, we sort of come to a fork in the road. He seems to've took the left hand."

"That's too bad. But he has a lot of company, these days."

I said regretfully, "I'm sorry, Colonel, that things don't seem to be workin' out the way they ought to for you. Anything Muley and me can do, we'd be tickled to try."

Austin shrugged. "There is a need for so many things, I would hardly know where to start."

"Well, sir, like what, for instance?"

He took a long, frowning look at the countryside around him. It was coming alive with the green of new grass and the bright splash of blue and yellow from bluebonnets and buttercups. "It's a beautiful land. I always thought Texas had the greatest potential of any land I ever set my eyes upon. And it does yet, I suppose, if only these warmakers would cease their everlasting talk of disunity and unrest."

"We live way off yonder in the far settlements. We don't hear much of what's goin' on."

"I imagine you hear enough. We have bad trouble ahead of us if we don't curb these restless spirits. For years I've preached that we should go our own peaceful way. And for years, the people would listen to me. But somehow I've lost control now. Other voices speak louder than mine."

"We've always listened to you, Colonel."

"I wish there were more like you." He studied us keenly. "How go things up on the Colorado?"

"Fair enough, sir. Moisture's good for the spring plantin'. Grass is risin' fine."

"I mean politically. Are they talking as restlessly there as in other parts of Texas?"

Uneasy now, I quit looking into his face. "Well, sir, you'll always find people like my brother. They're dissatisfied no matter what. We have Mexican neighbors, and we get along. The government don't bother us much out there. Too far for office-bred people to ride, I expect." I felt my face coloring. "Not meanin' any personal offense to you, sir. I mean, it's different with you."

Austin smiled faintly. "My friend. I had ridden horseback so many thousands of miles in colonizing Texas that a ride up the Colorado River would be like a Sunday picnic. Even now, I'm preparing for another trip to Mexico City."

"It's a mighty long way down there," I admitted. "Farther, even, than to Tennessee."

"Far in miles and in mind. I never look forward to that journey. It's like going to another world. But I have to. I want to reassure the authorities that we are loyal here. With luck, I may be able to persuade them to take action against some of the conditions which have caused grievances here. There are grounds for grievances; I would be the first to admit that. But we must have patience. The Mexicans move slower than we. Change cannot be rushed upon them."

I thought of the Hernandez family. "No, sir, it sure can't."

Austin gazed intently at me. "You're one of the older settlers here now. It's the old settlers I must depend upon to keep things from getting out of hand. Counsel with the new ones when you can—help them realize how precarious our situation is."

"I'll do all I can," I promised. But even as I said it, I

thought of Thomas. I thought how useless it would be to talk to my brother, or to anyone like him. I thought of Antonio Hernandez, too. He and his kind wouldn't listen any more than Thomas would.

"Mexico City," Austin repeated. "It's a long, long way. I hope I can be back again before the summer is out."

He wasn't. It was two years before we were to see Austin. He would come home a shaken and disillusioned man, no longer inclined to soothe the restless ones. He would come home from a long and unjustified imprisonment, certain at last that Texas had no future tied to Mexico, where all life depended upon the whims of whatever one man happened to have his fist gripped tightly around the whip of government.

Chapter Ten

Looking back afterward, we could see that war was as certain as the rising and setting of the hot Texas sun. It didn't explode suddenly like a shell. It built gradually step by step, block by block, as methodically as you'd build a church. But the comparison is a bad one, for this war was something out of hell.

Most of us "old settlers" denied its coming as long as we could. We wanted to plow our fields and work our stock and live our lives by our own pattern, and be left alone. But it inched up like a slow-building thunderhead, and we watched it the way we'd watch a storm cloud, hoping it would go around us instead of coming head-on. It came anyway.

On the one hand was the "war party" of Texians who wanted complete separation from Mexico. Some were honest in their fever for freedom; others were only looking for a way to grab new land, or hoping independence would allow them to gain title to the land on which they already squatted.

On the other hand were venal Mexican officials, greedy for personal riches and hungry for power, despotic not only with the Texians but also with their own people. Such men had a strong tendency to regard other people as little more than cattle, to be used for their own gain and driven and cast aside. Zacatecas and Monclova were only words to us then, but we were dimly aware that places of those names existed, deep down in Mexico, and that angry revolts had leaped to flame there. Clear up in Texas, we could smell the smoke. Santa Ana crushed those people with a red-smeared fist. Then his ruthless eyes turned northward. He had taken off his smiling mask. The sense of absolute power had gone to his brain like the fire of bad *tequila.* Now he was a stalking wolf that had gotten a taste of blood and liked it.

Mañana was an old Mexican word which translated into "tomorrow" but usually meant some dimly distant time that would never come. It was a lazy answer for the things that had not been done and might never be done.

But for Texas, *mañana* was almost here.

Ramón Hernandez had been on a trip to San Antonio de Bexar with his wife to show their baby to her parents there. She was already with child again, and soon she would not have been able to make the journey. It was no longer the dangerous trip it had once been, for Indians rarely showed themselves any more. Too many settlers had built their log cabins or their stone *casas* along the road. Still, there was always a nagging uneasiness about any traveler until he was home and safe. So I was relieved to see Ramón riding up to our field.

It had been three years since I had set foot on the Hernandez place. "The *Señora* Hernandez—Ramón's

mother—had gone to join the saints. I had not attended
the funeral because it would have meant I would have to
visit that house. I knew that just beyond the new wooden
cross stood one that by now would be darkened by time
and rain, a cross bearing the name *Teresa*.

On a trip to Bexar, Ramón had finally found a long-
sought woman who would be the mother of his sons.
Miranda was her name. She was tiny, like so many Mexican women, but she could move about like some kind
of a spirit, and do work that would break the back of
some larger women. What she may have lacked in being
a beauty, she made up by being a good cook. Ramón
had proudly brought her to our place several times before
she became *preñada* and could no longer make the trip.
Her meals were a feast after the bachelor cooking Muley
and I had endured so long.

What mattered most, of course, was that she was good
for Ramón. She could wrinkle her nose or wink her eye
and melt him like a slice of butter.

Ramón's Spanish ancestors had spent their lives vainly
hunting for treasure. Ramón was luckier. He had found
his.

Because she was so tiny, child-bearing was difficult.
There was a time when it appeared she might not live
through it. But she had, and the trip to Bexar was Ramón's reward to her for delivering him a son, and for
promising him another.

"What's the news in Bexar?" I asked after Ramón had
slaked his thirst out of my water jug.

Ramón didn't answer me right off. He was too busy
explaining to Muley why he hadn't brought Felix along,
or some of the younger brothers. Muley hungered after
company; he had had so little of it.

Ramón said finally, "Austin is back. It is said in Bexar
that he arrived in Velasco aboard the *San Felipe*." His face

creased. "It is also said that there was a battle in Velasco harbor, and the *San Felipe* captured a Mexican warship."

I felt a sudden angry impatience. "Why do they have to do it, Ramón? They play with firebrands in a powderhouse!"

Ramón waved the question away. "God made the animals to fight. It is their nature. I am afraid He made the man a little too much like He made the animals." There was acceptance in his eyes, but mixed with regret. "It is born in them. It is beyond them to be able to change the will of God."

"It's not the will of God that we go to war."

"He made men different from each other. He made them to talk different tongues and wear different-colored skins. A great many men have died for that, and that alone." He shrugged with a patience inborn in his people. "It is said that even the Colonel Austin talks now of war. It is said that even he—who always talked of peace—is saying that Texas and Mexico must free themselves of Santa Ana."

"He spent a long time in prison. A gentle man, caged up like an animal and for no good reason. It's enough to make him bitter."

"Or to make him realistic." Ramón's eyes were steady. "He is right, I think. There is far more Americans in Texas than Mexicans. Mexico has always had her Santa Anas. They run in the blood, like some disease passed down from father to son. We Mexicans expect it; we accept it. But you Americans will fight. I think you will cut free from it or die."

"If it comes to that, Ramón, what will you do?"

He gazed out across our fields of ripening cotton, our grain. He looked beyond to the cabin on the timber-lined creek. I could see the love of this land in his eyes.

Sadly he said: "Texas is my home. Yet, I am Mexican. I do not know what I will do."

Muley saw the two horsemen first. "Ramón," he called out, grinning broadly, "I thought you said Felix wasn't home. That's him comin' yonder, with Antonio."

They were riding fast. Antonio usually did; he had little regard for his horses. But somehow I could tell this time it wasn't just thoughtlessness. They rode with a purpose.

Anxiety leaped in Ramón's eyes. "Something may have happened to Miranda."

Antonio cut directly across our field, spurring his horse through our unpicked cotton and breaking down the stalks. Felix held up, starting to go around, then thought better of it and cut through after his brother. I thought, *There had better be a good reason.* I was angrier at Felix than at Antonio, for I would have expected this from Antonio any time.

Antonio pulled up. He had passed Muley without a glance. He flashed me a hostile look, then turned to Ramón. "Come, brother, it is time to fight."

Relief washed over Ramón. "Miranda is all right?"

"There is nothing wrong with your woman. But there is much wrong for your country while you stand here and talk with your *Americano* friend. It is time now for shooting, not for talking."

Ramón's eyes narrowed. "Antonio, you have been drinking."

"I do not drink when my country needs me. Fighting has begun, brother, *por allá*, in Gonzales. There has been a call for men."

Ramón's voice dropped to a whisper. "I had not heard . . ."

"You spent too much time on the road home from Bexar with your woman. You missed the news. The *Amer-*

icanos have a cannon at Gonzales, and they refuse to give it up. Against the command of Colonel Ugartechea, they have killed to keep it."

Ramón glanced at me, helplessness in his eyes.

Antonio said, "It is time to decide. Shall we bow down to this plague of locusts, or shall we offer ourselves as patriots? Felix and I have made our choice. What is yours?"

Ramón's face was stricken. "Felix? You would take Felix? He is still a boy."

"He will fight like a man!"

Ramón stepped up beside his younger brother's horse and put his hand on the boy's knee. "Felix, this is not for you."

Swallowing, Felix held his chin high.

I shouldn't have interfered, but I liked this lad too much to stand still. "Felix, you'd better listen to Ramón."

Felix would not look at me. Tightly he said, "Yesterday we were friends, Josh. Today we are enemies. I am a Mexican."

Antonio's eyes were like two black flints. "What are *you*, Ramón? The time has come to choose, and choose quickly."

Ramón shook his head. "Antonio, you are crazy."

Antonio spat in front of him. "I expected as much. Stay at home, then. Stay at home with your woman and your American friends. And when they have you in chains, remember that your brothers had the spine to fight!"

He wheeled his horse around and spurred back through our cotton. Felix paused a moment, eyes fixed on his older brother. He was wavering.

Ramón cried. "Felix, stay here."

But Felix touched spurs to the horse and went off in a lope.

And thus war reached us, even here in the far settlements on the Colorado.

I had a strong feeling now that Thomas would return. And I knew what he would be wanting.

That night Muley's dog set up a racket. Rifle in my hand, I eased the door open. On the front step stood a familiar figure, tall and angular. "Howdy there, Josh," spoke the surveyor Jared Pounce. "Might I be a-comin' in?"

Muley grinned broadly at the sight of an old friend. I said. "Sure, Jared. Come in and we'll fix you somethin' to eat."

Jared hesitated. "Josh, I got somebody with me."

His look made me uneasy. "Bring him on in."

Thomas Buckalew halted in the open doorway. He said nothing at first. We stared at each other in silence. Three years had passed since we had stood face to face. He appeared to have aged much more than that, for his eyes were grave, his cheeks brown and lean. I could see the beginnings of a silver glint in the long hair that touched his collar. He was too young for gray, but there it was.

Muley's grin had faded to fright. "Josh," he begged, "you fellers ain't a-goin' to fight each other again, are you?"

I said, "No, Muley, we won't fight." I stared at Thomas. "You've changed."

He nodded. "So have you, Josh. Been a heap of water flowed under the bridge."

We didn't shake hands. Neither of us was ready to make the first move, so it was not made at all. Too much stood between us—the bitterness of the parting, and the long empty years since. We had moved apart like the opposite branches of a tree, still bound by the common trunk but each grown in his own direction, away from the other.

Thomas said, "You been well?"

I nodded. "You?"

"Tolerable, I reckon."

The silence was long and awakened again. At length Thomas said, "I expect you wonder why I've come, after all this time."

"I think I know. It's the war, isn't it?"

Thomas nodded, his mouth drawn into a thin, taut line. "Santa Ana's sendin' up troops from Mexico under General Cos. They'll join Ugartechea in Bexar. If they come for us, and find us scattered, it'll be the death of us all. You've heard about the fight at Gonzales?"

"I heard this afternoon."

"The call had gone out for help. We got to band together and whip them before they pick us off one by one. I'm goin', Josh. I'd like you to go with me."

"Thomas, are you sure . . ."

"I know there's been a lot come between us, Josh. I know how you feel about what I done. But we got to quit fightin' each other now and fight together. Else it's all over for the Americans in Texas."

I already knew what my answer had to be, but I dreaded giving it. "Have you seen Colonel Austin?"

He shook his head. "I've talked to people who have. Jared can tell you."

Grimly Jared Pounce said, "They treated him real bad down in Mexico. He says we got no choice any more but to fight. He's goin' to Gonzales himself."

I clinched my fist. "I've got friends who'll be on the Mexican side."

Thomas said, "In war, a man's got no friends except those who are with him."

I glanced at Muley. "I couldn't take Muley. He's got no business goin' into somethin' like this."

"Muley can stay here. There's neighbors enough now to help watch out for him. Been no Indians in a long time."

"I guess you've got other men ready to go?"

Thomas nodded. "We'll all be gatherin' over at Noonan's. We'll ride for Gonzales in the mornin'."

I turned toward the wall pegs where my old flintlock rested. With it, I had brought down more deer than I could count. Now I would use it to bring down men.

"I'll go. Give me time to gather my plunder and talk to Muley. I'll go."

A carnival spirit prevailed at Noonan's. The old rogue was boasting loud and long, telling how he had foretold this trouble the first time a Mexican soldier had shot at him, years ago. He didn't mention what he had been doing to get shot at, and nobody seemed of a mind to ask him.

"They're a bunch of yellow cowards," he declared. "They slit a man's throat when they get the upper hand on him, but they'll squeal like a pig under a gate if things go agin them. Give us fifty good men and this war'll be nothin' but a horse race—them runnin' and us chasin'. We'll all be home and plowin' our fields inside of two weeks."

Old Noonan had never plowed a field to my recollection. The only thing I'd ever known him to raise was hell.

I took my blanket and walked away from Noonan's cabin. I stretched out on the ground by his corral, where our horses were penned. Presently Thomas came out and joined me. He said nothing for awhile. He sat leaning against a post in the darkness, drawing on his pipe and savoring the home-grown tobacco.

"Josh," he said finally, "it's been a long time since . . . since that girl died. Have you got over it all right?"

I shrugged. "I can think about her now without it painin' me so, if that's what you mean. It's only that now and again I get lonesome. I get to thinkin' how things would be now if . . ." I broke off.

"There's some single girls around. You haven't found yourself one?"

"I haven't been lookin'."

"Maybe you ought to. I think you need a woman, Josh. And likely someplace there's a woman that needs you."

I didn't mean to, but somehow I let a little of the old bitterness creep into my voice. "There was one once, remember?"

Thomas said, "She was a Mexican."

I knew he hadn't changed.

Chapter Eleven

We reached Gonzales too late to help, for the battle was over. The town's "Old Eighteen" had stalled the Mexicans for three days until reinforcements came from neighboring settlements. Then in a fog-shrouded wood on the Guadalupe, the Texians had touched fire to their cannon and watched it belch forth a load of scrap-iron balls and cut-up chain. Again and again the cannon spoke, the noise echoing and re-echoing up the river in the cool of early morning. When it fell silent, the Mexicans had gone, leaving behind them crippled animals and patches of blood.

The whole affair seemed an improbable parody now, on the face of it. I rode over to look at the cannon which had brought on the trouble. It was an ancient six-pounder mounted on oxcart wheels. In Gonzales, its main purpose had been to make noise that would scare off Indians. As a weapon of war, it wasn't much. As a cause of war, it was ridiculous.

But, of course, it hadn't actually been the cause. It had been only the spark which had touched off the powder. The fact that Ugartechea had heavy-handedly demanded its surrender and had sent an armed group to take it had been the final indignity, the last of a long series of insults against men of strong pride. The defiant band at Gonzales had stood their ground and run up a flag with the words *Come and Take It!*

Austin had said, "A gentle breeze shakes off a ripe peach. Can it be supposed that the violent political convulsions of Mexico will not shake off Texas so soon as it is ripe enough to fall?"

With this battle won, no one was sure just what should be done next. Men and horses and mules and wagons came pouring into Gonzales, ready for war. But no one agreed just how this war was to be fought. Angry talk and fist fights erupted. A dozen men who had been leaders in their own communities wanted to command this volunteer expedition against the Mexicans. Even narrow-gauge men like Noonan saw themselves as the ones to lead the crusade.

"I been fightin' Mexicans longer than half of you have been drinkin' hard likker!" he shouted at a group of us who had declined to acknowledge his leadership. "I'll take on any one of you now. Choose your weapons— knives, guns . . . I'll even fight you with a chunk of firewood."

I'd had a bellyful of his blustering. "Shut up, Noonan, or I'll get the wind out of you and you'll shrink to where a man could stuff you in a saddlebag."

Noonan railed at me, but I knew he wouldn't fight. The Phipps boys took his side. For a while it looked as though I'd have to do battle with both of them.

Thomas stopped it, the way he had stopped scraps of mine back in Tennessee. "You-all hush up now. We're here to fight Mexicans."

Austin arrived, and just in time. The fury died quickly. Austin was the man who had put these colonies on their feet, the man who had undergone bitter personal hardship and even imprisonment for our sake. Some of the fire-eaters had long preached against him because of his peaceable ways. But now we all gathered to listen. Always in the past we had turned to Austin for counsel. We turned to him now.

Seeing him came as a shock to me. He looked much older than when I had last encountered him, that day on the road near San Felipe. His hair was graying. His face was thinner than ever before, his shoulders stooped. Those strong eyes which used to look a hole through a man were melancholy now, and tired.

"Gentlemen," he said in a voice so quiet we strained to hear it, "we have come upon a bitter time. The tyrant has torn up the good constitution of 1824 which first established us here and started us toward prosperity. He has declared that from now on we have only those rights which he chooses to confer. We have striven for peace but have been given war.

"I know there are some among you who have differed strongly with me in the past. But let us put that aside and bind ourselves together. The salvation of Texas is in our hands. And, perhaps, the salvation of all Mexico. Let us fight for the constitution of 1824."

I heard Thomas speak out. "To hell with the constitution of 1824. Let's cut ourselves loose from Mexico. We'll write our own constitution."

There were some who agreed with Thomas, but the "old settlers" dominated the crowd. Their aim was not so much independence from Mexico as simply to rid themselves of Santa Ana.

Austin was not a well man. The mark of imprisonment lay like a shadow upon him. But hardship had been his constant companion these long years in Texas. He was used to it, and he granted it no concessions.

"We can no longer retreat," he said. "The die has been cast. We must fight and win, or Santa Ana will kill us as traitors."

A council of war was set up. Though Austin protested that he knew little of military matters, he was unanimously elected the general-in-chief.

"Very well, then," he said, and regret was plain in his gentle voice, "I shall except. And my first order is this: we march at daybreak. We march against Cos and Ugartechea. We shall go to San Antonio de Bexar."

And so we marched, our little "Volunteer Army of Texas." There were less than 400 of us at the beginning. And what an army! Our only uniform was a grim look of determination. Each man wore whatever he had, and most of us had only buckskins, darkened by long wear and smelling strongly of sweat and tobacco and smoke and rancid grease. The richer men—and they were few— wore boots or shoes. For most of us there were only moccasins. There were coonskin caps and Mexican sombreros, Kentucky longrifles and short-barreled muskets. Some men rode big, well-bred horses they had brought from the States. Most of us straddled raw Mexican ponies or mustangs, and a few rode mules.

Along the line we picked up volunteers—a pair of mustang runners here, a beehunter there. From Goliad trooped a group of dark-skinned Mexicans, stirred by reports of the bloodshed in Zacatecas and eager to join us against Santa Ana. Their arrival caused a ripple of un-easiness.

"Spies," Thomas gritted. "I never could trust a Mex-ican."

But they were accepted, for every gun would count.

With the group from Goliad—long called Bahía by the old settlers—came word that Texians had stormed the fortress there and had captured the Mexican troops, along with a large store of arms and ammunition left by General Cos on his march toward San Antonio. That was welcome news—as welcome as the arrival of Big Ben Milam.

I had never seen Milam before, but his name was heard often in the colonies. He was one of the "strong men" of the war party. He had agitated against Mexico for years. Only recently he had escaped from a Monter-rey prison and brought news to Texas of Santa Ana's invasion preparations. A tall man, he had picked up Mex-ican clothing somewhere along the way to replace the filthy prison garb. And because Mexican people were usually small, the clothes he wore were short in sleeve and leg. His scarecrow looks made it hard to realize the caliber of man he really was.

Travis rode in—another name I had heard often but whose face I had never seen. Six foot tall, blond, still in his twenties, William Barret Travis was a lawyer by pro-fession and a fighter by inclination. His name was at the top of Santa Ana's proscription list, for he had been bit-terly opposed to the Mexican government almost from the minute he had set foot on Texas soil four years be-fore.

Then came another whose name had conjured up many a legend. Jim Bowie rode into camp, leaving star-ing, whispering men in his wake. Fresh from Nacogdo-ches, he had pushed hard to get here before the fighting started. He swung down from a lithe gray mare, a big man in buckskins, that famous Bowie knife sheathed in leather scabbard, two pistols in his belt.

I knew him on sight. There could be only one.

Bowie looked older than I had expected, older than he really was. But I knew that if even half the stories told about him were true, he had lived a fuller life than a dozen ordinary men combined. The 'deep lines in his face, the dark pouches under his eyes, had been gained the hard way. Bowie had tried to drown himself in whisky after cholera had swept away his Mexican wife and family. *Borrachón*, they called him. The Big Drunk.

But now here he was, a strong man still, sober and ready to fight, ready to seek redemption at the cannon's mouth.

And Austin, still an *empresario* rather than a general, and despite his past disagreements with the sentiments of Milam and Travis and Bowie, was glad to see them in camp. He was a quiet man, a builder, and here he was out of his element. But these were fighting men. Austin badly needed their help to control his volunteers. They were eating up all their corn, drinking up all their whisky, killing for beef the work oxen that had pulled the Gonzales cannon all the way to Sandy Creek, then left it there, stuck.

Austin needed the peculiar talents of these three fighting leaders, and they were glad to oblige him. This was their line of work.

Probably none of the four suspected what was to come. Shortly, every one of them would be dead.

We came to Salado Creek, about five miles from San Antonio. Scouting parties went out to reconnoiter, but Austin made no move for an immediate attack on the Mexican force. We had visits by several delegates of the

Texas Consultation, which had been called so that the leaders of the various communities could decide what course the settlers would follow in their stand against Santa Ana. It seemed that with all the excitement the Consultation was having a hard time keeping a quorum.

Even Sam Houston, that towering giant of a man, vastly able and gloriously vain, came to make us a speech. He said that right now he thought we would do better to drill and prepare ourselves than to get tied up in a death battle with the Mexicans. After all, he pointed out, we were citizen farmers, not soldiers, while San Antonio de Bexar was fortified and manned by professionals. That was largely true, though most of us knew that a big percentage of the Mexican soldiers were actually convicts, serving their prison time in uniform instead of within stone walls. Their hearts would not be in it if they came against us.

This was pretty well proven true in the battle of Concepción. Austin called for Bowie and Captain J. W. Fannin, Jr., to take a detail of 92 men and find a good camp site as near the city as possible. I missed out getting into this bunch, but Thomas was with them. He had been restless as a caged cat, lying around camp. A chance to ride—anywhere—was as welcome to him as rain on new-planted corn.

He got more than he bargained for. Bowie and Fannin selected a place near the old Concepción Mission. It being late, they camped their men there for the night. Next morning they found they had been surrounded and were outnumbered by at least four to one. When the smoke cleared, the Mexican troops were in wild retreat for town, leaving their artillery and twenty to thirty of their men behind them dead. The Texian loss: one.

Thomas came back flushed with excitement. The battle had fired his blood like raw wine. "It was beautiful!" he declared, his eyes flashing. "If we'd just been able to get word back here and have the rest of you brought up we could have finished the whole thing. Bowie said we'd have tied Cos's tail in a knot."

The way it was, the situation degenerated into a kind of Mexican standoff. We had Cos and his troops bottled up in Bexar. He couldn't get out, and no help could get in. But our leaders were skeptical about taking us into that town against the Cos cannon, against those soldiers waiting behind the heavy stone and adobe walls. We sat . . . and we sat . . . and we sat.

Sitting, I think, was worse than fighting. Time got to be more cruel an enemy than the Mexican troops who watched us from the flat roofs and the church towers.

Of course, some men always find ways to occupy themselves. There were certain of the Mexican women in town who found the fair-skinned Texians not really so terrible. Sometimes at night they would come strolling out to assure the men that they weren't really that kind of women. And some among the men were always willing to prove that they really were.

Jacob Phipps had found himself one. "I don't care if we never go in there and fight them soldiers," he told us, grinning. "I'd rather just wrestle with Guadalupe." He gripped Thomas's shoulder. "Thomas, she's got a sister. Real little *tamale*, that one. All pepper. Come with me tonight. See for yourself."

Thomas gravely shook his head. With the same hard-shell pride he had always shown, he said, "I wouldn't dishonor myself. I would never pollute myself with a woman I wouldn't marry. And I wouldn't marry a Mexican."

I flinched, and he saw it. "Meanin' no offense, Josh. But it's the way I see it."

"None taken."

How could you take offense? He meant every word he said. You could get angry enough at a man like Jacob Phipps to pound his head against a wagon wheel, for he talked one way and acted another. But right or wrong, Thomas always did as he talked.

A few scattered skirmishes were fought, and finally one battle which got to be known as the Grass Fight. Bowie and a patrol of forty or so men jumped a Mexican pack train which they thought was bringing in silver to pay the soldiers. When the fight was over and the blood spilled, the packs were slashed open. There wasn't any silver. There was only grass, gathered to feed the horses.

That wasn't enough action to keep free men happy. Thomas paced restlessly in camp, a war fever burning in his eyes.

Every day the number of men became smaller and smaller. They were pulling out by ones and twos and threes, going home to see about the crops, going to comfort the wife and kids. The word we got in camp was that Austin wanted to march into the town and take it, but others were counseling against him. The longer he waited, the more desertions he suffered, the lower sagged the troops' morale.

I'll admit that if it hadn't been for Thomas I'd probably have pulled out like so many others did. I thought often about Muley all by himself out on the place, probably scared half to death. But Thomas was duty-bound to stay. All hell couldn't have pried him loose.

Word came from the Consultation. Austin was being sent to the United States to try for money and men. We didn't know it then, but he would work so hard on this mission that he would wreck his already frail health, and he would die without seeing the full fruit of his labor.

It looked as though we were going to lose the siege of

San Antonio de Bexar by deterioration, rather than by battle.

On the fourth of December—two months after the cannon had spoken at Gonzales—Ben Milam walked among the discouraged men who still remained. A grim determination was in his eyes, and in the hard set of his jaw. Danger was an old acquaintance of his. They had never been far apart since the first time he had set foot in Texas nearly twenty years before.

His strong voice challenged us: "Who'll go in with Old Ben Milam into San Antonio?"

By twos and threes, by tens and twelves, men rose to their feet and reached for their rifles. Thomas spoke not a word, but he tucked the old Kentucky flintlock under his arm and felt for his shot pouch and powder horn. He glanced at me, his eyes asking the question.

"I'll come along," I said.

Commander Burleson had taken over after Austin left. He didn't like Milam's move, but he gave us the support of his artillery, dropping cannon balls into an ancient, half-ruined mission which the Mexicans had long ago turned into a fort. Cottonwoods stood around this once holy place, and around the high stone walls which surrounded it on all but a part of one side. Because of this, the mission had long since lost its church name and had become known by the Spanish word for cottonwood: *Alamo*.

There were some three hundred of us, divided into two companies. Ours was under Milam, the other under Colonel F. W. Johnson. We were outnumbered by three to one.

Six long, hard days we fought. It was toe-to-toe battle, and we moved by inches. Again and again the din of gunfire became so loud that I thought my head would explode from the pain of it. The sharp smell of gunpowder was always there, and the smoke kept my lungs afire. Now and again my hair would bristle at the death scream of a mortally wounded man on their side or ours.

The Mexican soldiers were tired and hungry and scared, but give them this: they fought like men. Surrounded, they could not run. So they stood and fought, and every inch of ground we gained was soaked by someone's blood. Crossing open streets was suicide. Rather than suffer terrible casualties by frontal assault, we bludgeoned our way toward the enemy's strongpoints by taking battering rams and plowing through the stone and adobe walls.

We moved on room by room, house by house, for most of these Mexican houses were built one against another. We would grasp the heavy poles used for rams, swing them a few times for momentum, then drive them into a wall. Sometimes women and children would scream in terror as the wall crumbled away and they stared at us through the swirling dust. Sometimes there would be Mexican soldiers in these rooms. Rifles would roar, knives would flash, clubs would swing viciously, and men would go down never to rise again.

But slowly we made our gains.

The cost was high. The third day, Ben Milam stepped out into the street, and a bullet struck him in the head. He never knew what hit him.

At last we had the crumbling old Alamo itself under our guns. Rifleshots crackled, cannons roared, and dust and gunsmoke hung heavily in the air. Our battering ram smashed through the adobe wall of a small Mexican house. For a second I glimpsed brown faces and excited black eyes before the guns flashed red and bullets went whining. For a minute it was as if we had torn open a hornet's nest. Then, all lay quiet. In the room only the dust and the smoke still moved, suction drawing them out through the gaping hole. Half a dozen of us stumbled into the room, our rifles ready to fire again. Crumpled on the floor lay five Mexican soldiers, all of them dead but one, and he mortally wounded. He cried out weakly to Holy Mary, the Mother of God. I don't know what drew my gaze to the slight figure slumped in a corner. Even before I saw the face, I felt my heart skip.

I dropped to one knee and gently turned the body over. I could tell at a touch that life was gone. A mass of blood had welled out of two holes in the front of the dirty shirt.

I knew that begrimed, crimson-smeared face.

Felix Hernandez.

I knelt there a long moment, my throat tightening as if a huge fist had clamped over it.

I heard Jared Pounce's quiet voice behind me. "Friend of yours, Josh?"

I nodded. "A kid is all he was. I've known him for years."

"Too bad," the old Texian said sympathetically. "He ought to've been on our side."

"At his age," I replied, "he oughtn't to've been on anybody's side."

I pulled at a small chain and found the crucifix Felix had been wearing around his neck. It would be the only thing of value he had on him. The family would want it for remembrance. Carefully I removed it and put it in my pocket.

"Looky yonder," I heard Jared shout. "Look at the Alamo. There's a white flag goin' up!"

I stared in disbelief, but there it was, rising to the top of a pole, the breeze catching it and flapping it wildly. The gunfire slowly died away. And in its place came the wild, jubilant shouting of the Texians.

"We've won! We've won! They're givin' up!"

Six days of hell had ended. I slumped to the dirt floor of the little house and leaned back against the adobe wall, exhausted, numb. Within reach of me lay the body of Felix Hernandez, but I couldn't bring myself to look at him again.

Why couldn't they have raised the flag an hour earlier?

I had thought I knew what it meant to be weary, but until now I never really had. I was sick of San Antonio, sick of fighting, sick of the sight and smell of blood.

A sharp chill had come. The light clothes, the single blanket were no longer enough, for this was mid-December. I stood beside Thomas as we watched Cos march out of San Antonio on the road that led south to the interior of Mexico.

With him went the remnant of his troops. In two weeks there wouldn't be a hostile Mexican soldier left in Texas.

I had looked up Antonio Hernandez among the prisoners after the battle. I had tried to tell him about Felix. He heard me—he had to—but he gave no sign of it. He refused to look at me, to answer me. His face was like something carved out of stone. He was with the troops as they moved south.

"Thomas," I said, "it's over. I'm goin' home."

Thomas shook his head. "It ain't over, Josh. It ain't hardly even begun. They'll be back, and next time there'll be more of them than there was before."

"What do you figure on doin'?"

"There's some of us that want to go down into Mexico and carry the fight to *them*. Burn their towns, spoil their land."

"Thomas, weren't the last few days enough for you? Haven't you seen enough blood spilled to last you for a lifetime?"

Again he shook his head. "It's them or us, Josh. We're not half done fightin'."

I wrapped my blanket around my shoulders and looked off toward the Colorado. "I've had enough. I'm goin' home."

I had almost rather have taken a whipping at the hands of Santa Ana himself than to have to go to the Hernandez house with the message I carried. I took Muley with me, for he had stuck to me like a bur. Like a pup whose master has been a long time gone, he would not let me out of his sight.

We rode the familiar trial, and I dreaded the first sight of that stone house. When it came in view, I could see that very little had changed in the three years since I had been there. I reined my horse to a stop and looked at the place a long time, trying to get my courage up. Old memories came racing through my mind, memories I had forcibly buried long ago.

Muley looked at me worriedly. "How come we stopped. Josh? I thought we was goin' in."

"We're goin' in, Muley. It's the hardest thing I've ever had to do, but we're goin' in."

The dogs greeted us a hundred yards from the house and gave us a noisy escort. The younger Hernandez kids came running out, shouting joyously. I stepped down and handed the reins to Muley.

"You stay out here with the little ones, Muley. I'll go on in and do what I've got to do."

I gripped the crucifix nervously in my fist. I look a deep breath, then walked up under the brush arbor to the front door. The door swung inward. The breath all left me.

"Teresa!"

The girl at the door stared in surprise, then slowly shook her head. "Not Teresa. It's been a long time since we've seen each other, Josh Buckalew. Don't you know me?"

It was a minute before the shock left me so that I could answer. "María?"

"Yes, I am María. I've changed since you saw me last. You've changed too, Josh."

I could tell that in some ways she looked like her sister, and in other ways she didn't. The swift first impression had brought the image of Teresa back to me, María was not quite so tall. She was pretty, but she didn't have quite the fragile beauty of Teresa. María looked stronger, surer of herself. I doubted there was anything fragile about her.

"The wind is sharp outside, Josh. Come into the house."

I found myself trembling a little. "I'm sorry if I look like a fool. It's just that, for a second or two, you gave me an awful start."

"I would never take you for a fool, Josh. Please, come on in."

I followed her. Now Miranda came out of the kitchen, drying her hands. On her tiny frame her pregnancy was showing strongly now. It wouldn't be many months before Ramón would have another son—or a daughter.

"Josh Buckalew," Miranda smiled, "this is a surprise. After all these years, you've finally come to see us. I thought you were off to war."

"I was. Fighting is over now. I'm home again."

The two women looked quietly at each other. "It is over?" María said. "Then perhaps Antonio and Felix will be coming home."

My fist tightened on the crucifix. "Miranda, where's Ramón?"

"He rode out to find a horse. He should be home in a little while."

María pulled out a leather-bottomed chair. "Please,

Josh, sit down. Tell us about the fighting. Was it terrible?
Were you wounded?"

Gratefully I took the chair. I looked at the dirt floor.
"Yes, it was terrible. No, I was not even scratched."

"And it is over now? All the men will be home?"

I shook my head. "Not all the men."

It seemed an eternity before Ramón finally came. I
had to keep answering the women's questions while trying not to let them see in my eyes or sense in my voice
the message I had come to give them. When I could, I
stole glances at María. She was a woman now, not a girl.

At last Ramón came. I gathered all my courage and
told them about Felix, and Antonio. I held out my hand
with the crucifix in it. I saw María's eyes flood with tears
before she turned away and buried her face against a
white-plastered wall. Miranda clutched Ramón's arm as
he took the crucifix from my hand and tenderly ran his
fingers over the raised figure.

"I wish there was something I could say, Ramón, besides that I'm sorry."

Ramón's voice was brittle. He did not look into my
face. "Thank you, Josh, for coming and telling us. Now,
please, I would like you to go."

Chapter Twelve

Muley and I finished the scrapping that was left on the little bit of cotton he had not already picked. Later we planted a crop of wheat for spring harvest. It seemed there was always too much work to do.

We saw nothing of Ramón Hernandez. I dreaded any return to his place, and he evidently felt no wish to visit us. I could imagine his heavy sense of loss and knew it was not unreasonable to assume that he attached blame to me. I had been part of the attacking force.

The war news we received was scant and mostly contradictory but strong rumors kept drifting in that Santa Ana was gathering an army in Saltillo. How large it would be was something we could only guess at. Many Texians were not prone to worry, for they felt sure one American could whip ten Mexicans. After San Antonio, I didn't believe this—if I ever had.

In any case, no one thought Santa Ana would start

north before spring. We all figured it would be late March or even April at the earliest before his troops would wet their feet in the Rio Grande.

In the meantime, precious little was being done to get Texas ready. Wrangling in the privisional government left it impotent. Personal feuds and jealousies kept it going in futile circles. Our Texas army was small and badly scattered, ill-disciplined and ill-equipped. Worse, its officers were quarreling among themselves just as the officials of the government were doing in San Felipe. Sam Houston had the command—on paper—but not many of the subordinate officers paid much attention to him. The command was splintered.

It was at this time that Travis, sharing a command with Bowie in San Antonio, wrote to Governor Smith that the people were "cold and indifferent . . . and in consequence of the dissensions between contending and rival chieftains they have lost confidence in their own government and officers." He added with disgust: "The thunder of the enemy's cannon and the pollution of their wives and daughters—the cries of their famished children and the smoke of their burning dwellings only will arouse them."

And that was the way things stood when Santa Ana's advance guard crossed the Rio Grande on the twelfth of February, six weeks to two months earlier than anyone really expected.

He caught us scattered, quarreling and totally unprepared.

The first word of Santa Ana's advance was much worse than I had any idea it would be.

It was brought by red-faced old Alfred Noonan. Though any Mexican pursuit had been left days behind him, he spurred into our yard as if Santa Ana were reaching for his shirttail.

"Josh Buckalew!" he shouted. "You better go see about your brother!"

I never had felt any respect for the old man, and after the battle of San Antonio I had only contempt. I couldn't remember ever seeing him at any time when the action was heavy. Only when the conflict was over did he present himself, and then he was blustering and posturing as if he had won the battle by himself.

I walked out into the yard to meet him now. I didn't want to offer him any favors, but I could tell that his mount had been badly used. I pointed down toward the creek.

"Muley, go water Noonan's horse for him, will you?"

Noonan stepped down and handed the reins to Muley. "Much obliged." Noonan's face was flushed even more than usual, his eyes bloodshot.

"Now," I said, "what's this about Thomas?"

Noonan swung his arms in a wide gesture. "Old Santy Ana's done crossed into Texas with the biggest bunch of Mexicans that you ever saw in your whole life. He's acomin', Josh. There ain't nothin' goin' to stop him but the good Lord Hisself, and the way things are goin' He must be busy someplace else."

"What about Thomas?"

"Boy, I'm afeered your brother is wounded. Maybe dead. There was a scrap down on the Rio Grande. A little bunch of our boys got caught by them Mexicans. It was like a panther pouncin' on a mouse. Most of our boys got theirselves kilt. Thomas was with that bunch."

Ice touched the pit of my stomach.

"You sure. Noonan? You're not just scared and excited?"

"They was down there, him and the Phipps boys and some others. Was all fixin' to go and raid Matamoros, but the orders never did come through. So they stayed down there and watched along the river. I was supposed to've been with them, only somethin' else come up."

Bet your life it did, I thought darkly. You hid.

"Jacob Phipps come back, shot in the arm. He said he seen his brother Ezekiel get his head blowed off. The last he seen of Thomas, he was ridin' off into the dust and the smoke to where the big shootin' was. There was an awful scatteration after that. A few of the boys like Jacob come a-limpin' back. Most of the others never did. Far as I know, Thomas didn't."

"As far as you *know*?" I grabbed him by the shirtfront. "Didn't you try to find out?"

"Boy, them Mexicans was a-commin'! I'm tellin' you, they wasn't like any Mexicans I ever saw. They was thousands of them, and they was lookin' for blood!"

The terror of it was still naked in his eyes. I realized the old fraud couldn't help himself. Like many a big talker, he had feet of clay. I let go of him and stepped back, my heart sinking.

"If Thomas did come back, Noonan, where would he most likely be?"

Noonan shrugged. "Hard to say. Maybe Bexar, where Travis and Bowie are at. Maybe Goliad, because Fannin is there, and we was sort of under Fannin's command there towards the last."

I clinched my fists. For a moment hopelessness swept over me. Surely Thomas was dead.

And yet again, he might have gotten out.

I knew what Noonan's answer would be before I ever asked him. "You want to go back and help me look for him?"

Noonan shook his head violently. "No, sir, thank you. I had enough Mexicans to do me for the rest of my life. I'm takin' the Sabine chute!" That was a way of saying he was heading for the Sabine River and the safety of the United States.

"You got a farm here," I pointed.

"Old Santy Ana can just have it back."

I was too dumb to offer him anything to eat, and he was in too much of a hurry to have accepted it. Soon as Muley brought his horse back, Noonan spurred away. I leaned my shoulder against the log cabin and stood there weekly, watching him disappear over the hill.

"Muley," I said, "I got to leave you again."

Muley cried and begged me like a little boy. But I had no choice except to leave him here. I couldn't take him with me into God knew what.

"Muley, you listen to me, and listen tight. There's no tellin' when I may get back. If the Mexicans come—and they may—don't let yourself get caught by them. You run. Take the best horse we got and run just as fast as you can. If you have to cross the Sabine, you do it, and don't stop to look back. When this is all over, I'll come find you."

"Josh," he cried, "I don't know what I'd do if you was not to come back."

A lump came in my throat. I wasn't sure either what would ever become of Muley. Alone, he would be as helpless as a child.

"I'll come back."

"You promise, Josh? You promise you'll come back?" His eyes brimmed with tears.

"I promise, Muley. Now you take good care of things while I'm gone. And remember what I said. Watch sharp. Don't let the Mexicans find you here."

It was now past the middle of February. Riding for San Antonio de Bexar. I found people still not certain what to do. Some were packing their belongings and getting ready to head east. A few were already on the road. But most were waiting, still hopeful that the Texian forces could turn back the assault.

I rode into Bexar a little less than three months after I had left it. The city still showed all the scars of the awful battle, many of the stone and adobe houses caved in, gaping holes knocked in their sides by cannon balls or battering rams. I rode along the main street and found to my amazement that despite the dozens of rumors that Santa Ana's column was not far from the city, business still went on more or less as usual. Most of the stores were open, peddling whatever stocks they still had after the December disaster.

I rode up to the high old stone walls of the Alamo and found them fortified. If it came to the point of making a stand, I thought, Travis would probably pull his men into the mission. Its enclosure was big and rambling, containing more than two whole acres. In that respect it would be hard to defend with a small force. There was an alternative: the Concepción Mission, where Bowie's men had first come into conflict with the Cos troops back in November. But Concepción was outside of the city. The Alamo was the more likely choice.

A familiar voice called my name, and I looked up at the wall. There stood the tall, stooped figure of Jared Pounce.

"Howdy, Josh!" the old surveyor shouted. "You come to help us fight Santy Ana?"

I waved back at him and pointed to the open front gate. Jared climbed down and met me there as I rode in. We clasped hands. "Jared, you're lookin' good. To me, you always look good."

He smiled. Somehow I could tell he hadn't been smiling much. "Then I look better than I feel." His smile

gradually left him. "I reckon you know what's comin',
Josh."

"I've heard rumors. All of them bad." I grasped his
arm. "Jared, is Thomas here?"

He shook his head. "No, is he supposed to be?"

I knew I shouldn't feel disappointed. I hadn't really
expected to find Thomas in Bexar. But the disappointment was there, just the same. I told Jared what Noonan
had told me. Jared listened solemnly.

"Josh, I think you better make up your mind to accept
it. Thomas is likely dead."

"There's still the shadow of a doubt. Jared. I can't stop
lookin' till I know for sure."

"I was hopin' you'd stay here with us. We'll be needin'
all the men we can get."

A short way along the wall I watched Travis supervis-
ing the building of an embankment for emplacement of
a cannon. The strain of command had left its mark. He
was impatient and snappish with the men doing the work.

Jared said dryly. "He's tryin'. But he's fussin' with the
wrong men. The ones he needs to crack the whip over
are out in town, enjoyin' theirselves. Seems like the men
are ready to fight and die with him, but they ain't willin'
to follow his orders."

Across the courtyard came big Jim Bowie, walking un-
steadily.

"Drunk?" I asked Jared.

"He's been drinkin' a little. Mostly he's just sick. Needs
to be in bed. He and Travis don't get along, but they
have to put up with each other. Half the men here won't
listen to anybody except Bowie."

Travis and Bowie fell to arguing almost as soon as
Bowie reached the embankment. They were too different
to be able to get along. Travis was a gentleman born.
Bowie had acquired the manner of a gentleman, but he

had come up in a rough-and-tumble world of brawling and dueling and wild adventuring. Beneath the polish he was still a backwoods-man.

Their quarreling would soon end, for the enemy was almost at the gates. Then they would stand together, shoulder to shoulder, and leave the world a legend that would never die.

Jared Pounce shook hands with me again at the open gate of the old mission. He said again. "I wish you was stayin'."

"I can't. I expect I'll go next to Goliad. Thomas could be there."

"If you don't find him, come back. The Alamo walls are high and stout."

None of us had a premonition then of what would so shortly come to pass. I did remember, though, that one reason General Cos had surrendered his Mexican troops to us in December was that he considered the Alamo indefensible.

Even now, most of the old Texians were not thinking in terms of independence. They were thinking only of defeating the despot Santa Ana and getting a fair shake from the Mexican government.

Jared said, "Josh, I been doin' a lot of thinkin' lately about what I'm goin' to do when the fightin' is over. You remember, it was me that showed you the place that you boys settled."

"I remember."

"There's still some land close by open for settlement. I think when we get the shootin' finished and square our-selves with Mexico, I'll take up some land out there and be neighbors with you. I always did like that country along the Colorado."

"We'll look forward to it, Jared."

I glanced back once as I rode away and caught a last look at the lean old man there by the front of the Alamo. I would never forget it.

The road from San Antonio to Goliad roughly paralleled the San Antonio River. I set out from the city without delay, for I had a strong feeling there wasn't much time. And there wasn't. Not far from San Antonio my horse suddenly pricked up its ears. It turned its head a little to the right, and I glanced in that direction. I saw horsemen, ten or fifteen of them. Texians, I thought, on their way to join Travis's garrison. Then I caught a glimpse of blue, and I knew. These were Mexican cavalrymen.

They saw me about the same time I saw them. There was no point in trying to do battle with that many men, even if I had had the inclination, which I didn't. It was a horserace for awhile. But eventually I lost them somewhere in the timber.

So they were here. I had been lucky in running into this bunch, then getting away. I was still alive, and free. At least now I knew I had to be alert.

I knew I would have to do a lot of hard riding and very little resting until I reached Goliad.

I learned something else, too. The lesson was abrupt and unexpected. I rode up to a Mexican house, expecting to ask for a fresh drink of water, for this was a place where the trail had dropped back away from the river. What I got was a blast from an old *escopeta* in the hands of a Mexican farmer. He missed me, but he taught me that from now on I had to avoid habitations.

A good percentage of the Mexican people in Texas disliked Santa Ana. But he had proclaimed this a holy war, Mexican against American. It was, he said, a racial war, dark skins against the light. Other matters of politics were put aside for the duration of this crusade. A great many of the Mexican people who otherwise opposed him accepted this at face value because they basically disliked Americans even more than they disliked the little Napoleon of the West. Now that Mexican troops were in the country again, I could not afford to trust any Mexican—civilian or soldier.

From this point on, I moved carefully, leaving the road and skirting any houses I came to.

The old presidio at Bahia, generally known as Goliad by the time of the Texas revolution, had changed hands often, usually with violence. It had been a pawn in the Mexican war of independence against Spain. Its grounds had been tramped by the boots of filibusters. Last October it had been wrested from the Mexicans by Collinsworth and Milam. Now it was probably the chief Texian stronghold, for James W. Fannin had between four and five hundred volunteers quartered there.

The town had once held a thousand or so inhabitants, but now most of its brush *jacales* and its mud and stone houses stood empty. The Mexican people had withdrawn from this place of contention to the comparative safety of the *ranchos* down the river. A scattering of abandoned mongrel dogs roamed its deserted streets, hunting for enough food to keep themselves alive. Cattle blundered in and out of the doorless dwellings, some of which had already caved in.

Built on solid rock atop a hill, stood the presidio itself, its thick stone-and-lime walls weathered to an oppressive gray by the long years. A chapel stood in the northwest corner, fronted by an artillery emplacement. The parade grounds were all enclosed by high stone walls which ran south and east from the chapel. This was the finest fort the Spaniards had ever built in Texas, for it straddled an important road from Nacogdoches to the interior of Mexico, and it was also near the sea. If there was a fort which could hold out against Santa Ana, I thought, this would be it.

Soldiers stood along the walls and out in front. One patrol stopped me briefly but quickly let me go.

Riding into the fort, I was struck by the fact that most of these men were not actually Texians. A majority were volunteers fresh in from various Southern states. Something else struck me, too—the strong faith in these men that they could whip anything that came along.

"Bring any Mexicans with you?" somebody shouted at me. "We're ready for a fight."

I explained my mission and was taken directly to Colonel Fannin. He didn't give me time at first to ask about Thomas. He insisted on hearing how things stood in San Antonio, and back in the settlements. I told him San Antonio had still been open when I had left there. Then I told him about running into Mexican cavalry. His face creased. He paced, his hands behind him.

"How many did you see?"

"Just a patrol, ten or fifteen."

"You saw no others? You saw no columns?"

"Nothin' but that patrol. Other than that, all I can tell you is the rumors I've heard. You've likely heard those already."

He frowned. "A hundred of them, and no two alike. We are in darkness here. We don't know what's going on to the south. For that matter, we know very little that's going on to the north and east. We're isolated. Sometimes I think they've all forgotten us."

"I doubt that's so, sir. One story I've heard is that a lot of men are gatherin' in Gonzales. Buildin' up an army. I expect General Houston will take command of them if it's true. And they'll most likely be marchin' in this direction."

Fannin still paced. "I hope so. Meanwhile I wish they'd let me know what's going on. I wish I could tell just what to do."

I told him it looked to me like this fort was situated to stand off a big siege.

Fannin nodded briskly. "You know how Mexicans fight. It'll take a lot of them to dislodge us. We'll never give up the ship while there is a pea left in the dish."

I nodded agreement, but it occurred to me he was overconfident, like his men appeared to be. The Mexican troops he had seen so far had seemed amateurish and even comical to his West Point-trained eyes. He was downgrading them too much. That could be a costly mistake.

"Colonel," I said, "I've come looking for my brother. I wondered if he might be here."

I explained to him what Noonan had told me. Fannin went to his duty rosters and slowly ran his fingers down the pages, shaking his head as he came to the bottom of each one.

A chill passed through me. I knew before he had finished what his answer had to be. "I'm sorry, there doesn't seem to be a Buckalew listed here anywhere."

I swallowed. "Colonel, does what Noonan said sound like anything you've heard of? Do you know of any scrap that fits the description?"

Fannin rubbed the back of his neck.

"Our reports from down that way have been very sketchy, Buckalew. There could have been a dozen engagements and we wouldn't have heard of them." He turned to a big Texas map which had been pegged to his wall. His finger sought out Goliad. "Now, it's possible your brother could be attached to Johnson's force at San

Patricio." His finger dropped south on the map. "It is highly probable that Johnson would be keeping patrols out south of San Patricio, possibly all the way to the Rio Grande. And, if the Mexicans have crossed in force, it is likely that some of these patrols have made contact with them. Violent contact." He turned and faced me. "If you're going that way, I hope you find him alive. And, Buckalew," he paused, "if you find out what the Mexicans are up to, find a way to get the information to me."

"I'll do what I can, sir." I left him then and started for San Patricio.

Chapter Thirteen

It was all strange country to me, for I had never been in this part of Texas before. This was the coastal region. When the wind was out of the east I could smell the Gulf, or fooled myself into thinking I did.

I wasn't interested in seeing the country, though. My immediate concern was to get to San Patricio without falling into Mexican hands. I followed the trail, for without it I wouldn't know the way. But as on the road to Goliad, I took pains to skirt around any Mexican dwellings.

I came at last to a house that was plainly American-built. Here, at least, I would be welcome. I rode up to it boldly.

That turned out to be a grievous mistake. A Mexican civilian stepped into the yard, a blunderbuss in his hand, and fired at me without so much as a howdy-do. I wheeled the horse around and spurred away, thankful for fast horses and poor Mexican marksmanship.

That was my second such experience. Santa Ana's race war idea had taken hold. I knew now I would have to live by Thomas's old credo: never trust a Mexican.

There were creeks along the way: Blanco, Medio and some that weren't named on the map one of the Goliad officers had sketched for me. The rations I'd carried with me from Goliad gave out and I ate dry bread until I came across a fat cow, caught and butchered her. Taking some of a hind quarter, I rode a long way before daring to stop and cook the meat.

I had lost count of time, but I knew it was the last of February or first of March when I ran into the three stragglers.

They could have been Mexicans, for all I knew. I drew off the trail and into a clump of timber, covering my horse's nose with my hand, hoping they hadn't seen me. My rifle was cradled in my arm, ready. The horseman came directly toward me, one slumped forward, another helping hold him in the saddle.

Their horses sensed mine. One of them nickered. Instantly two of the men slid off onto the ground, thrusting their rifle barrels up over their saddles. They could have been either Mexican or American. I held my breath and brought my rifle to rest across the branch of a tree. My hand tightened on the stock.

One of the men shouted, "Grab Bill. He's fallin' off."

The man who had been slumped was sliding out of the saddle.

The voice had been enough. They were American. I shouted, "It's all right. I'm a Texian." They still didn't trust me. I led my horse out of the timber and dropped the rifle down to arm's length to show I wasn't hostile. The two men on their feet still kept their rifles pointed at me. I saw that one—a man with red hair and a tangled red beard—was holding his leg out stiffly. A dried crimson spot showed on the dirty cloth wrapped around the leg. The wounded man in the saddle had a gray coat bundled around him, one sleeve dangling empty. Bloodstains showed he had been shot deep in the shoulder.

"It's all right," I repeated. "I come from Goliad."

They lowered their rifles. One said, "Lord, it's sure good to see a friendly face. I hope to God you got somethin' with you a man could eat. And maybe a little water? Bill here is burnin' up with fever."

I helped them lower the wounded man to the grass and brought my canteen. While I carefully doled out water to the one named Bill, the other two hungrily tore into what was left of the beef.

"It's been much hidin', little water and no rations for us since them Mexicans hit us at San Patricio," one man said, his jaw bulging.

I looked up sharply. "San Patricio?"

"They came on us unexpectedly. Killed nearly every man. I never thought there was so many Mexicans."

"I was on my way to San Patricio. Lookin' for my brother."

"Mister, if he was there, I expect he's dead."

"His name is Thomas Bucaklew. Do you know him?"

The man frowned, thinking. "Buckalew? I don't believe I recollect such a name as that. There wasn't no Buckalew at San Patricio, was there, Red?"

The red bearded one stopped chewing. His lips moved as he formed the name quietly to himself. Then he said, "I seem to remember there *was* a Buckalew, but not at San Patricio. He was south, with a patrol that worked down all the way to the Rio Grande."

Excitement began to build in me. "Where would he be now?"

Red shook his head. "In heaven, I expect, or in hell.

Most of the boys down on the river were killed by the first Mexicans that crossed over."

"Did you see anybody who said they saw him die?"

"No, but there was only a handful came out alive."

I looked south, my eyes narrowed. "He could be down there someplace hidin' out, maybe wounded. I might be able to find him."

The bigger of the two men said. "You'd be throwin' your life away to try. You know that country down there? Ever been there before?"

I told him I hadn't.

"Well, there's nothin' down there now but Mexicans, thousands of them. They caught even the boys that knew the country. You would go down like a rabbit in a wolf's den."

It took me a long time to decide to turn back north with these three battle survivors. I could think of a dozen reasons why I should go on south, but these man had an answer for every one of them. They stressed that it was unlikely Thomas could still be alive. That I could find him was even more unlikely. And to fall into a Mexican trap was almost certain death, for Santa Ana's orders were to kill.

"I seen one boy that lost his horse throw his hands up and try to surrender," said Red. "They shot him to pieces."

"That's why you got to go back with us," argued the other, named Jimson. "You got no chance atall. And besides, we need help with Bill."

My jaw went tight when I looked down at the worst wounded of the three. He wouldn't live to reach Goliad. That bullet had been in him too deep, and too long.

So when all the talking was done I had to turn my back on Thomas and San Patricio. I had to accept the probability that Thomas had fallen with the others, and

that even if he hadn't, there was nothing I could do for
him.

Only three of us lasted to reach Goliad. We scratched
out a shallow grave for Bill and left him near Blanco
Creek. We led his horse on in. At a time like this, horses
would be worth more than gold.

Nobody paid much attention to me, for hardly anyone
in the fort at Goliad knew me anyway. Most of them
hadn't been in Texas more than a few weeks. They were
volunteers from the States, for the most part, come to
whip the breeches off a bunch of dirty Mexicans. Besides,
I hadn't been in any of the recent fighting. But the men
thronged around Red and Jimson, eager for details of the
battle.

"Battle, hell," Red snorted, favoring his leg. "It wasn't
no battle. It was slaughter."

Colonel Fannin sent for us as soon as he heard. We
found him in his quarters, worriedly studying a map. He
frowned at me. "Aren't you the man who was here looking for his brother?" I said I was, and that I hadn't found
him. Fannin nodded sympathetically, as if he had known
all along that I wouldn't. He turned gravely to Red and
Jimson. "I've already had the bad news from San Patricio. But I'd like to hear it from your viewpoint."

They gave it to him briefly and simply. They didn't
have to embellish it any, for the truth was bad enough.
Fannin questioned them closely about the Mexican
strength. They could only guess, for like the field soldier
anywhere, their knowledge of the war was limited to what
went on in front of them. The war, to them, was whatever their own part of the battle had been. And for Red
and Jimson, it had been bitter.

Fannin said, "There weren't enough of you, and you
had no position of strength. So, the Mexicans took you.

Here we have one of the best fortifications in Texas, and adequate men to defend it. When they get here, we'll stop them cold. I can use you men—all three of you—if you'd care to stay."

Red gingerly touched his leg. "I'm tired of ridin' with this. I'd sure admire to rest. And I doubt there's a safer place anywhere than Goliad." Jimson agreed. Fannin looked at me.

I nodded, grimly accepting what had to be the truth. "I'll take up where my brother left off. And here is as good a place as any to turn and fight."

So, without ceremony, we were marched into Fannin's command of volunteers inside that gray, grim stone fortress on the hill.

Fannin believed in drill, and he tried to carry it out in West Point style. It honed the discipline of a military command to a fine edge, he said. We were well honed, for we had several hours of it every day. Some of the volunteers complained that they had come all the way from Georgia and Kentucky and Tennessee to fight, not to drill. They drilled anyway. And when we weren't drilling, we were busy strengthening the rock walls, building new emplacements for artillery.

I was at the gate the day a courier came downriver from the direction of San Antonio and spurred up the hill on a worn-out horse. Stiff and weary, he almost fell from his mount as he reined to a stop. I helped grab him. On his feet, he leaned back on the sweat-lathered animal.

"Colonel Fannin," he gasped. "Message for Colonel Fannin."

I said. "We'll take you to him. Where did you come from.

"From San Antonio de Bexar. The Mexicans have gotten there."

"How bad is it?" somebody asked.

"Bad. Travis. Bowie and the others, they're forted up in the old Alamo. Travis sent me to fetch help."

We took him to Fannin's quarters. The courier braced himself with a strong shot of whisky while Fannin read the message from Travis, his brow furrowed. At length he said.

"My last orders were to hold Goliad. If I split my force to go to Bexar, I would jeopardize our position here."

The courier argued, "They're goin' to need help if they hold the Alamo."

Fannin's sense of futility showed plainly as he turned and looked at his map. He ran his finger along the road from Goliad to San Antonio de Bexar. "Ninety miles to San Antonio. Even with a forced march it would take us time to get there if we took the equipment we need." He rubbed his hand across his face. "I wish to God I knew what to do."

I thought he was going to make a decision, but he didn't. He said he needed time to think. He ordered us to leave while he continued to talk with the courier.

Later, Fannin made his decision. Against his better judgment he ordered us to prepare for a forced march to the relief of the Bexar garrison. We hadn't gotten far before we had a breakdown. Still not certain he had done right, Fannin was discouraged. Somewhere to the south— and probably not far—was a strong Mexican force. If it caught us on the road, we might have a hard time fighting through. The officers counseled.

Fannin reversed his decision. The order came to retreat to Goliad. It was a foregone conclusion now that the Alamo would not stand. Better to stay together and hold Goliad, Fannin declared, than to risk the loss of all.

So James Bonham, the courier, disregarded the admonitions of all around him and spurred once again toward San Antonio to carry the bad news to Travis:

Fannin wasn't coming. He could have stayed. To return was death, and he knew it. But he went.

It was a cold grim, gray day when the expected news came from San Antonio. The Alamo had been overwhelmed. The garrison had been slaughtered to the last man.

Even expected, it was a staggering thing. Travis, Bowie. Crockett, Bonham, and all those others . . . men we had fought beside, men we had eaten with and drunk with.

And for me there had been someone special, old Jared Pounce.

A pall of gloom descended upon the garrison at Goliad.

Yet the strange thing was that few really thought it could happen to *us*. Not here at Goliad. When the Mexicans came we'd show them how Americans could fight. We'd repay them for the Alamo.

What began to break our back was the division of our forces. Word came from the village of Refugio, some thirty miles east toward the Gulf, that families there wanted to leave and needed an escort. Fannin sent Captain King of the Georgia Battalion and a company of twenty-three men. Reaching Refugio, they found themselves hard pressed by Mexican cavalry. They took cover in an old mission. A messenger managed to break through the Mexican lines and reach Goliad. This time Fannin sent out Colonel Ward with the Georgia Battalion of about a hundred and fifty men to relieve King.

We didn't know it then, but there men would never come back. We expected their return at almost any time. But a day passed, two days, and still no word.

Then came a courier from San Houston, bearing orders to Fannin that we abandon Goliad and retreat to

Victoria, to the area of heavier American settlement.

Had we followed the orders when they arrived, things might have turned out differently. But Ward and King were still out. We couldn't just abandon them. We were told that Fannin was restlessly pacing the floor of his quarters, trying to decide what to do. He was between a rock and a hard place, between military obligation to his commanding officer and the moral obligation he felt toward the men he had sent out and had not heard from.

So again we waited . . . one day, two days, three days. The Mexicans weren't waiting.

At last Fannin found out for certain what we had all begun to feel in our bones: Ward and King and their commands had been taken.

Fannin gave the order to prepare for evacuation. We worked through the night packing up and getting ready to be on the move. We mounted the artillery that we could transport. The heavy artillery, we spiked. The rest we dumped into the trenches we had sweated so hard to dig, and we covered them up. We set fire to everything that would burn.

With daylight we set forth into heavy fog on the road to Victoria, two hundred and fifty or so men afoot, about twenty-five a-horseback, a company of artillery, nine small pieces of ordnance and a mortar, all drawn by oxen. Because I had a horse, I was attached to Colonel Horton's scouts. We rode ahead to the ford on the San Antonio River, half expecting attack there, for we had seen Mexicans and had even had a scrap with a Mexican patrol. The attack didn't come, but the largest cannon stuck in the river. We lost an hour pulling it out of the mud.

In all the bustle, nobody had thought to feed the oxen. They were hungry and contrary. All in all, it started out to be a hard day.

We were well across the prairie about ten miles from Goliad, and the oxen were still giving trouble. Ahead of us lay Coleto Creek and a heavy stand of timber. But we came across a patch of new grass in an area that had been burned over by the prairie fire. Fannin decided we had better rest and graze the oxen, or they might never get us to the timber. So another order went down the line: stop and unyoke.

I didn't like it, but nobody asked me. Somewhere—not far away—there had to be a large force of Mexicans. We had seen enough of their patrols to have no doubt about it. Even so, few of the men seemed overly worried. There was still that powerful conviction of our own superiority. Most of them agreed we couldn't be beaten by a ragtag bunch of greasy Mexicans.

Our scouting group went out to look around while the command rested. We didn't go far, and we didn't see anything. When we returned, the oxen were yoked again and the march resumed.

We could camp when we reached the timber, the officers agreed.

We never made it. A vague dark line began moving up in timber to the south of us. As it detached itself from the timber, we saw that the line was made of horsemen, and many of them. We looked back. Behind us came another line. Both lines approached rapidly and began spreading out.

"My God," Jimson shouted, "there are thousands of them!"

There weren't, but there were enough to take a man's breath away. We began crowding the oxen, struggling to make the timber.

Colonel Horton shouted an order. One of the six-pounders was quickly unlimbered. A shot was fired at the horsemen, and another, and another.

"That'll scare them off," the colonel said hopefully.

But all three rounds fell short. The Mexicans kept coming.

Our rear guard came galloping up. We pushed on a little farther. The ammunition cart broke down. We lost time while men transferred the load. By then the Mexican cavalrymen had circled around to the front of us. They had cut us off from the timber.

"Circle up men!" Fannin shouted. "Circle up!"

Some of the volunteers began firing their rifles, but the range was still much too long. Fannin ordered the shooting to stop. No use wasting powder and lead. We formed a hollow square, facing our artillery outward to fire on the enemy from whatever direction they might come.

Now we could make out the horsemen distinctly. We could see the flying pennants. We could hear bugles in the chill of the March air.

They sounded what must have been the charge. The Mexican cavalry spurred toward us from three directions. Our artillery opened up with grape and cannister shot. We could see horses and men go down. The Mexicans kept coming, right into the range of our rifles and muskets. We began to fire, timing ourselves by ranks so that one group was in position to shoot while another was loading. Great gaps were blasted through the Mexican ranks. Still, on they came.

Their forward riders were upon the square itself when the rapid and deadly fire of our volunteers stopped them. The Mexicans reeled back, loose horses running wild, stirrups flapping ... wounded horses threshing and screaming. Mexicans afoot looked around desperately for comrades to pick them up. Some were abandoned and fell under the Texian fire.

While the Mexicans pulled back, we reloaded and surveyed our own damage. It was heavy. We had already lost most of our horses and oxen. We had several men killed and a number wounded.

To my dismay I found that the man named Red lay lifeless behind one of the cannons, a gaping hole in his chest. He had taken a bullet through the leg at San Patricio but had survived to rejoice that Goliad would be safe for him. Now he was dead. The irony of it was bitter.

Before this was over, he would turn out to be the lucky one.

Overconfidence appeared to curse both sides. The Mexicans evidently had expected to sweep over us with ease. The steel-coated resistance of these volunteers had come as a deadly surprise. They feinted at us several times, but they kept falling back as soon as they reached rifle range. They quit trying to charge and set up a constant fire of muskets and *escopetas*. We answered their fire. Some of the Mexicans began crawling toward us, hiding in the tall dry grass. But a lot of our volunteers were crack riflemen. Any time they saw enough of a man to draw a bead on, they usually hit their mark. The Mexican losses were heavy.

The fire continued until nightfall. Then the enemy withdrew to the timber. That gave us time to look around and consider our situation. The longer we looked, the less we liked it.

Ahead of us, so near and yet so far away, stood the timber we had been trying for. Once in it, we could take advantage of its cover and stand off a force several times our size. Out here in this open prairie, we were paralyzed.

But how could we ever reach the timber now? In the growing darkness we could see the wink of Mexican campfires around us. Our teams were gone, either stampeded by the gunfire or killed by it. The officers took tally and found that we had seven men dead, sixty wounded. A majority of these wounded would be unable to walk.

Among the wounded was Fannin himself. He had taken a rifle ball in the thigh.

What water we had with us was gone. Most of the ammunition for our cannons was used up. Food supplies were scanty, for the officers had felt confident we would reach Victoria and had not wanted to overload the wagons.

Now night fell upon us, cold and terribly dark. I still had my blanket, but I found that many of the men had dropped theirs when the fighting started. Now they were without. I tucked my blanket around a wounded man who lay shivering from the cold. He cried for water, but I had none.

Fannin called the men around him. Calmly he outlined the seriousness of our situation, something most of the men had become painfully aware of already.

"We still have a chance," he said, "to reach Coleto Creek and the timber. The darkness will help cover us. And I think that if we run into Mexican troops we can fight our way through. But we'll have to go afoot and there are many among our wounded who cannot walk. We can go, and we can reach safety. But if we go, we'll have to leave those who cannot make the journey afoot."

Someone said, "Colonel, what will the Mexicans do to the men we leave?"

Fannin minced no words. "You all heard the report that came to us about the few of Captain King's men who surrendered a Refugio. They were taken out and shot."

"That means," the soldier declared, "they'll probably shoot anybody we leave behind."

Fannin said, "That is the way it appears to me. We can save ourselves by leaving the badly wounded behind to die. Or, we can stay with them and all take our chance together. I won't command you to do either. I'll leave it up to you men to take a vote."

There was a minute or so of hushed conversation among the men. Almost every one of them had a close friend or relative among the wounded. The decision was unanimous.

"Very well," said Fannin, and I could tell that he approved the decision. "We'll stay. We'll build whatever fortifications we can during the night. And then we'll see what the morning will bring."

Chapter Fourteen

The night was long and black and cold. The groans of the wounded raised the hair on the back of my neck. Not even in the battle of San Antonio last fall had we been involved in a situation as desperate as this. In their fever, wounded men begged for water that no one had. The little bit of water had long since been used up. All of us thirsted, but for the injured the night was torture. A light mist hung in the air, though not enough to afford relief. On the contrary, it made the cold bite deeper.

Hungry, cold, sleepless, those of us who were able worked through the night digging trenches, fortifying ourselves the best we could. It was too cold to rest long at a time. Instead, we worked.

When we had the ditches two or three feet deep, we dragged up the oxcarts and the carcasses of horses and oxen, and placed them for breastworks. Through the long night we listened to the Mexicans blowing their bugles, far out in the darkness. If it was an attempt to keep us awake, they needn't have bothered. We were too cold and hungry and thirsty to sleep. Once in a while a Mexican sentry would cry out, *"Sentinela alerta,"* a sign that all was well. For them, it might have been.

Daylight finally came. It was Sunday, March 20. As the darkness began to fade, we could see the Mexicans moving. Three or four hundred men were coming up as replacements, bringing with them a hundred or so pack mules. They had two new brass nine-pounders and would certainly have a fresh supply of ammunition.

The cannons roared. We threw ourselves face down into the tramped-out grass and dirt. The shots were too high. They were over our heads. Fannin, wounded and in pain, gave the order to hold our fire. "The range is too great, and our ammunition is too low. Let's wait until we can hit what we shoot at."

The Mexicans fired their cannons several times, not a single shot hitting inside our tight square. Again movement started among the ranks of the Mexican cavalry. We brought up our rifles and muskets, sure the charge was about to commence. Instead, an officer rode out, carrying a white flag.

"Maybe they want to give up," somebody said dryly.

One of our majors and some other officers walked out to meet the Mexican about halfway between our position and the enemy lines. They talked a little, then came back. The major went straight to Fannin.

"That's General Urrea's command out there. The general sends word that he wants to avoid shedding blood without reason. He guarantees that we'll be dealt with leniently if we surrender at discretion."

Fannin exploded. "At discretion? That means unconditional. That means we retain no rights. We turn ourselves over to them to be treated in any way they see fit."

The major nodded solemnly. "I reckon that's what it means."

Fannin looked at us then, his gaze slowly sweeping the whole miserable little band huddled behind the embankment of earth and the upset carts and dead animals. He shook his head. "Go back and tell him we shall *not* surrender at discretion. We had rather die to the last man in these trenches!"

The major delivered his message. The Mexican officer wheeled his horse around and carried the report to General Urrea. Shortly the whole Mexican line began to move again. It looked once more as if the charge would start at any moment.

Instead, a handful of men rode out toward the truce area. Jimson whistled. "Look at the uniform on that Mexican. That must be Urrea."

Fannin, propped against a pack, his injured leg extended in front of him, lifted a spyglass to his eye. "It is Urrea indeed. He wants to parley. Major, I guess this time I had better go. I'll need your help." The major and half a dozen of us moved quickly to aid him.

Fannin, on his feet but favoring the wounded leg, turned and looked again at those of us gathered around him. "Men, I suspect that this time he has a better offer, or he wouldn't have come. I know that as commander I am supposed to make the decisions. But this may mean your lives, and I'll not make the decision alone. If you choose, we'll stay here and fight until we die. But if you vote to surrender, and we are offered acceptable terms, I shall abide by your vote. What say you?"

The officers huddled first. Then they divided us into our own companies for a quick discussion.

When the question came around to me, I said, "Either way, we lose. We're trapped here. If we stay we'll either starve or be killed. We can't break out without leaving the wounded, and the longer we stay the more wounded there'll be."

Jimson took it up. "We couldn't leave the wounded. So it comes to this: we stay here and die for certain, or surrender and hope."

I pointed out, "You know what happened to King's and Ward's men who surrendered. They were shot."

Jimson shrugged. "A chance of war. If it was an easy decision, we wouldn't be standin' here arguin' over it."

In the end, the decision was made. We would surrender if Fannin could get us good terms. Otherwise, we would stay here and die like the men of the Alamo had died.

Fannin went out, the major and some of the other officers with him. Every step he took was agony.

After a long time, Fannin and the major came back. And with them came the resplendent General Urrea himself, bringing several aides. They wrote down the agreement, a copy in Spanish and one in English. All signed it. Fannin folded the English copy and put it inside his coat.

So we gave up our arms and marched out of the trenches, carrying our wounded with us.

It was a slow, painful, pride-killing return to the fortress we had left. Nobody talked much, for the shock and hurt went too deep. Most of these men had come to Texas lightheartedly looking for the grand adventure, the great crusade, to strike a blow for liberty and show a contemptible enemy how Americans could fight.

It was all for nothing. They could fight, these volunteers, but they had been wasted by poor planning and indecision and a fatal contempt for the enemy. The cause was good, the spirit strong; but it had all been thrown away.

The officer who had superintended the surrender of

weapons was a German mercenary. Many of Santa Ana's officers were Europeans. In good English he said, "Well, gentlemen, in ten days it will be liberty and home!"

It sounded good at the time. But it would come back bitter as gall.

They put us in what had once been the chapel, and we began to wish we hadn't worked so hard to destroy everything in the fortress before we left it. That first night was torture. We were crowded so tightly that not all had room to lie down. The trapped air was hot and stifling. We gasped for breath.

Our wounded needed attention and fresh bandages, but the Mexicans had few or none for themselves. Contrary to the terms of the surrender agreement, which had guaranteed to respect private property, the Mexican soldiers methodically robbed us of whatever individual possessions we had. In my case, it wasn't much. I had already lost my horse, my saddle and my blanket.

The wounded suffered severely for want of attention. The Mexicans had taken our few doctors away to treat their own men. Gangrene developed in some of the wounds. The stench and the moaning of the men made cold sweat break out on the rest of us. We had water now, for details were permitted to go down under guard and fetch it from the river. But there was little food, and no chance to make broth for the men who so badly needed it.

Some of our wounded passed away, and death came to them as a friend.

It was the following Friday that a call went up.

"More prisoners!"

The gates opened. More than a hundred men dragged in—I couldn't say they marched—and the gates closed behind them.

"It's Major Ward," one of the officers declared, and hurried forth to meet the new prisoners. With Ward was the tiny remnant of his men who had survived the battle at Refugio. In addition there were a hundred or so fresh volunteers, taken at Copano the minute they stepped down from their ship. They never had a chance to take a rifle in hand, much less to fire it.

Their faces were sad, angry, frustrated. They had tried, and they had failed. Now they were at this dreary hell with us. I couldn't bring myself to look at them. I dropped my gaze, staring at my dirt-crusted moccasins, my ragged breeches.

I thought I heard someone call my name.

"Josh?" It was more a question than anything. I raised my eyes, and my heart leaped.

"Thomas!"

I jumped to my feet and grabbed him. We hugged each other, blubbering like children. At last he groaned, and I saw what I had overlooked in my haste and my joy. He was wounded. His tattered coat was buttoned with his left arm inside, the sleeve hanging empty.

"Thomas," I cried in relief, "I thought you were dead."

He looked as if he wanted to smile but couldn't. "I thought for a while that I was too. Damn it, Josh, I hate to be a-findin' you here."

"I'm glad to find you here, or anyplace. I'd given you up."

Thomas's eyes showed pain. "You shouldn't have gotten yourself into this. You ought to've stayed home."

"Old Noonan came by the place. Said he thought you'd been wounded, or killed. I set out to find you."

Thomas gritted, "Noonan, that old scoundrel! Big talk, but a yellow streak as wide as your hat. Time for fightin' come around, he wasn't to be seen." He looked at me again with those sad eyes. "I'm sure sorry to find you here."

I said, "Where were you? How bad is that wound?"

He shrugged, and the effort hurt him. "I was south of San Patricio. On patrol. The Mexicans caught me by surprise. Killed most of the boys. They shot me in the shoulder, then killed my horse. He fell on top of me. They left me there for dead. I finally got out from under the horse and started walkin' north. It was mighty slow going." He looked around. "Josh, I sure hope you got somethin' here to eat. I'm starved."

I shook my head. "There's not much. We've all been hungry for days. A few of the boys managed to hide away a little coin when the soldiers looted us. They been buyin' a small bit of bread and coffee from the camp followers. Outside of that, the Mexicans have been bringin' us a little beef . . . nothin' more."

Thomas found an open spot by the stone wall and dropped down to stretch his legs out in front of him. He flinched as pain from the bad shoulder grabbed him.

"Thomas, you better let me look at that shoulder."

He waved me off. "The bullet's out. Time will take care of the rest of it. If we've got any time."

"What do you mean?"

"These Mexicans haven't been takin' prisoners."

I told him we had a guarantee from Urrea. Colonel Fannin still kept a copy of the agreement in his pocket, as far as I knew.

Thomas asked, "Where is Urrea now?"

"He left. Went on to wherever the fightin' is. A colonel by the name of Portilla is in charge now."

"Urrea signed the paper, and now he's gone?"

I nodded. Thomas grunted, then dismissed the subject. He started asking me how things had been at home when I left. I told him all I could.

It was strange how all our past differences faded away under these cruel gray walls. Whatever bitterness might have lingered in me had disappeared in my relief at seeing him. The trouble we shared now, the oppression of captivity, made us brothers again.

Thomas told me how he had wandered afoot after the battle, the wound causing a fever that set him to staggering, half out of his head. An old Mexican found him, took pity on him and carried him to his *jacal*. There the old man and his wife dug the bullet out of him. They hid him for days while Mexican patrols scouted for stragglers.

"Josh, I always said I'd never take a favor off of a Mexican, but that pair saved my life. I owe them more than I could ever say. If I get out of this alive, I'll find some way to pay them. If I don't get out and you do, I want you to pay them for me."

"Thomas, you'll get out. The war is over for us. They say they're goin' to send us home."

He grimaced. "Maybe." He told me the old couple's name and how I could find them. "You remember now, I want you to see that those old folks don't ever need for nothin'."

I agreed, to get him to quit fretting. "Sure, Thomas, if it comes to that. But we're both goin' to live. If the Mexicans take Texas away from us, we can always go home to Tennessee. And we'll go together."

Chapter Fifteen

Palm Sunday, March 27. It was a beautiful morning, bright and shining with the hope of freedom. Some of the friendlier guards had brought us the rumor that a ship was being sent to Copano to take us on board and carry us to the United States. A feeling of vast relief had swept gloom from the prisoners' compound. Now there was rising jubilation.

"Home," the man said. "They're sendin' us home!"

Last night we had all sung, "Home, Sweet Home," and the words brought tears that burned many an eye.

We didn't know that as we sang, a courier arrived from Santa Ana. The general had flown into a black rage when he learned about Urrea's prisoners. So the courier had brought Colonel Portilla a written order that the officer crumpled in horror. We didn't know the colonel had paced in his quarters all night, racked by conscience, praying for forgiveness for what he had to do.

*   *   *

The gates opened. We stood up—those who could—hoping the guards had brought beef. Instead, a Mexican officer stepped into the yard and signaled for us to gather around him.

Thomas was stiff and sore from his wound. I helped him to his feet. He leaned on me for support a moment, until he had the strength to walk alone.

"Good news, my friends," the officer said. His mouth was smiling, though it struck me that his eyes were not. "You are starting home today. The ship is arriving in Copano. You have but to walk there."

More than three hundred voices lifted in a lusty cheer. I shouted with them, then glanced at Thomas. I saw hope flicker in his eyes, but I saw doubt there, too.

The officer said. "Those who are able to walk will do so. The badly wounded will stay. They will be taken later in carts. It will be necessary for guard purposes to divide you into groups."

He picked out our officers and told them to gather us into their own commands. Because Thomas had been captured alone and belonged to no group here, I kept him with me. The men who had been captured as they got off the ship at Copano had been given white armbands to wear while they were in the fortress. Now this group was all gathered in one section.

I saw Fannin lying on the ground, unable to walk except with the greatest pain and difficulty. He was smiling as he watched us. The Mexicans up to now had not honored all the terms of the capitulation. They had allowed their soldiers to rob us. They had not fed us as they had agreed. But now they were sending us home. Fannin, I thought, must have felt gratified about this. It meant that after all his defeats, at least he had made a decent bargain for us.

"Thomas," I said, "you'd better stay here. Let them bring you in a cart."

He shook his head violently. "I'll make it. I want to get out into the clear air."

I had some serious doubts, but I figured if he gave out they would let him ride.

I got to thinking then about Muley, back there at our place. Not much telling what would happen to him now. It seemed a certainty that the Mexican army would over-run everything in its path. If he didn't run, they would catch him. If he did run, where would he go?

We were marched out the gate, one group at a time. Ours was the third to leave. The last—the men with the white armbands—were still inside. As we moved out into the open, it struck me that spring was coming now. The brush was leafing, the grass turning green. The sky was a light, clear blue. I didn't remember when I had ever seen it so beautiful.

They started us down toward the old ford on the river, Thomas kept looking back over his shoulder.

"Funny thing, Josh. They didn't bring the other two bunches this way."

"What do you mean?"

"They took them off in other directions. This is the road to Copano."

I didn't have an answer. I looked at the armed Mexican guards who marched on both sides of our strung-out line, an uneasiness stirring in me. About a hundred volunteers were in our group. The other groups which had gone out before us had been much the same. There weren't as many of the guards as there were of us. That didn't look like treachery. And yet, Thomas's contagious suspicion began to work on me.

Several Mexican cavalrymen leisurely worked their

way down on horseback from their encampment, carrying lances under their arms.

Jimson was in fine spirits. "They must be figurin' on proddin' up the slow ones. But goin' home, there ain't nobody apt to be very slow."

We walked along in silence. I kept watching Thomas now, and I saw his suspicion gradually change into alarm. He turned now and again, counting the guards over and over, seeing where they were. His restless eyes followed the lancers.

"Josh," he said quietly, "if worst comes to worst, the lancers are the ones you got to watch. Half of these guards probably can't shoot. But those lancers will sure run you through."

"Thomas, you're just borrowin' trouble."

"I'm talkin', that's all. But you listen, and listen good. There's lots of brush along the river. A man could hide himself in there, if he ever made it that far. With luck he could hold out till dark. Then he could head out across country. He'd have a chance to get back to our own lines and maybe strike another blow at Santa Ana."

He walked along hunched a little, for the shoulder was hurting him. I said, "You ought to've stayed and ridden in the cart, like I told you."

He shook his head. "If we're really goin' to Copano, I'll make it. If we're goin' to die, I'll die out here where the air is clean."

"Thomas, you quit talkin' about dyin'."

"You remember what I said about that old Mexican couple. See after them, you hear?"

I wondered how he figured—if something was going to happen—that I would live through it and he wouldn't. I guess he knew that with his bad shoulder he couldn't run far.

We had walked about half a mile from the fortress

when a Mexican up front raised his hand and shouted. *"Alto!"* We all stopped.

Jimson called in high good humor, "Tell him we're not tired yet. Tell them we want to keep on a-walkin'."

Several commands were given in Spanish. The squad of guards on the upriver side of us began to move. They split, half going around in front of us, half in back of us. In a moment they filed up to join the guards who were stationed between us and the river.

Thomas stiffened. I saw his face turn a leaden gray.

Then, from far off in the distance, came the ragged sound of musketry.

Jimson gave voice to the sudden horrible realization that swept over us all. "My God, boys, they're goin' to kill us!"

I heard someone cry out. Men began to pray. One man dropped to his knees, his head bowed. Someone shouted, "Rush them, boys! It's our only chance!"

Thomas clutched my arm. "The river, Josh! The river!"

Some of the men began to run toward the Mexicans, hoping to overwhelm them. At a command the soldiers raised rifles to their shoulders. I stood paralyzed, my mouth dry, the cold hand of death holding me there in horror. I looked down the barrel of the rifle that was going to kill me.

Thomas moved suddenly. He stepped directly in front of me. The rifles roared. The impact slammed Thomas's body back against me, men fell like wheat beneath a scythe. I could hear the thud of bullets driving into flesh and bone. Some men died without a sound. Some cried out in mortal pain. I clutched Thomas, but my hand was sticky and warm. I knew instinctively that he was already dead.

For a moment I lay there—half pinned down by his

weight—numb, unable to move, to think, to speak. Around me men still prayed and cursed and moaned and died.

Then the realization came to me that I was still alive. I had not even been hit. Thomas had taken the bullet that would have been mine.

And it came to me that men who had been missed by the volley were beginning to run. There had not been enough rifles to kill us all with the first shots. More by instinct than by conscious will, I lay still. I lay there and looked into Jimson's open, dead eyes.

The Mexicans were reloading their rifles as rapidly as they could, many of them moving awkwardly forward as they rammed powder and ball down the barrels. In pursuit of those men who ran up the hill, they moved over us and away.

This was my chance, if I had one at all. Stealthily I eased out from under Thomas's weight. I gripped his hand, saying a silent good-bye, my heart pounding. Then I jumped to my feet and sprinted toward the river.

A ball whizzed over my head. I cut sharply to the left and ran even faster. I glanced back over my shoulder, half expecting to see a mounted lancer bearing down on me. I was lucky, for they were all busy elsewhere. But I saw a rifleman drawing a bead. I cut to the right. Again a ball missed me.

Then there was the brush. I plunged into a thicket, the branches and the thorns clutching at my ragged clothes, ripping into my skin. I could hear a horseman loping toward me. I glanced back and saw him coming, the lance tipped forward.

I would make it tough for him, catching me in this brush.

Something struck my left arm. It felt like a red-hot poker. I reached up with my right hand and touched the arm and felt the thin flow of blood. I had been nicked by a rifle ball. But I kept on running.

I pushed through the brush until I reached the steep river bank. They were still coming behind me. I dived. The icy-cold water paralyzed me a moment. Then I started to swim. My first thought was to try to make the opposite bank, climb out and keep running. But the current was swift. I let it carry me along and only treaded to keep my head above water. I kept trying to look back, to see if I was being followed. So far as I could tell, I wasn't.

In a few minutes the current carried me to a spot where the opposite bank was not steep, and where a growth of old grass would hide whatever marks I might make as I climbed out. I clambered over the bank as quickly as I could and tried to lose myself in the timber. I dropped down on hands and knees in a heavy growth of underbrush, clutching my arm, feeling the warm trickle of blood. My heart was still in my throat. I could hear firing across the river as the Mexicans found and murdered one after another of the unfortunate volunteers.

The terror of it swept over me in a spasm of shuddering. Unable to control myself, I lay flat on the ground, clenched my fists and let the bitter tears flow.

When I was able to collect my wits, I realized I was alive but a long way from being free. It was still less than a mile back to the fortress, with many open stretches of prairie to cross whenever I tried to move farther away. Riders splashed across the river. I could hear the horses grunt as they labored up the bank. They were coming toward me. I huddled in the thicket and prayed softly.

I heard the sound of running feet. Thirty yards away a young volunteer was pounding through the brush as hard as he could. The lancers came yelping eagerly be-

hind him, like hunters after a fox. The youth screamed,
"No! God, no!"

The first lance impaled him. A second caught him and
drove his body to the ground. The lad gave one horrible
cry. One of the soldiers got down, put his foot on the
body and pulled the lances free. Another soldier dismounted. Together they stripped the dead man of his
clothes, laughing as if this were a sporting event, and they
had just killed a deer.

Now I could hear firing in the fortress itself. The
wounded! They were killing the wounded—Fannin and
the rest.

More than three hundred helpless men—slaughtered
like cattle!

I had not had time to feel anger. There had been only
fear, and horror. Now came the anger, a bitter, driving,
helpless rage. I pounded my fists against the ground.

I knew now that I *had* to get out of there.

Thomas, I swore, *someday, somewhere, somehow, there'll come
a day of reckoning for this. And I vow to you and Almighty God,
I'll be there!*

Soaking wet, hungry, bitterly cold, I huddled in the
brush all that day. Now and again patrols passed through
the timber, hunting for stragglers. I stayed low. My arm
stiffened and burned, but at least it was no more than a
deep scratch. The ball had taken a bite of flesh and
passed on. I would live. Or at least, it wouldn't be this
wound that killed me.

I tried to decide what I should do. Even with the best
of luck, it would be difficult to escape from here. With
any bad luck at all . . .

I had no hat, no coat, only these ragged clothes between me and total nakedness, with the chill of winter's
breath still lingering into spring. My moccasins were thin.
They probably wouldn't survive a long walk home, or

even farther if the Texian line had retreated beyond it. And if there even was a Texian line. For all I knew, the Mexicans could already have swept to the Sabine River.

I knew that without food I would never get far. I'd nearly starved for a week now on the meager ration they gave us in the compound, and today there had been nothing at all. I wondered about the deserted Mexican *jacales* in the town of Goliad. I might find something there, if I had the nerve to go and look. A coat, a blanket—something. Probably no food, for the people had been gone too long. They had fled downriver last fall to the scattered *ranchos*, where they thought they would be safe from the war. Maybe if I could get to one of the *ranchos* I could steal some food and some clothing.

I had never stolen anything in my life, but now I was going to try without the slightest twinge of conscience. What did it matter? They were just Mexicans, I told myself. I realized I was thinking the way Thomas had always thought.

Well, he was dead now, and Mexicans had killed him. Maybe he had been right all the time, and I had been wrong.

I knew from description where the *ranchos* lay. My clothes had fairly well dried out through the day. Still, I was chilled to the bone. Even walking, I couldn't get warm. So most of the time I kept going, for the cold hurt me worse than being tired.

I had no firm plan, other than to try to sneak into a house and get some clothes to wear, some food to take along. Ahead lay a small rock house, very much like the one the Hernandez family lived in. Around it were scattered several brush *jacales*. A lingering smell of woodsmoke touched my nostrils. My stomach growled, for woodsmoke meant food.

Dogs were one thing I hadn't counted on. It never occurred to me they would pick me up so quickly. They set in to barking and raced out to meet me with a noisy clamor.

"Hush up," I hissed at them. They didn't savvy English. I crouched behind a bush and tossed rocks at them, trying to scare them away. They didn't scare. Presently a man appeared in the doorway, an ancient musket in his hand. I backed away in the darkness without his seeing me. I couldn't go up against that musket. Maybe there would be another house, one without dogs.

A mile farther on, I saw it. I moved in slowly, expecting the same reception. But this house was quiet. No dogs. I approached stealthily, flattening myself against the rock wall. I eased myself up to the open window and listened. Inside, a man was snoring.

It was somewhere past midnight, I didn't know where I had heard it, but a dim recollection came to me that someone had said people sleep soundest in the hours just after midnight. If that was true, I had a chance here.

Something moved beside me. My heart flipped. I jumped a couple of feet, whirling to face whatever it was.

In a square crate made of green willow branches I saw a rooster, one of the fighting breed so beloved by the Mexicans. I had disturbed his rest. I swallowed hard, regaining control of myself.

The door was closed, but it moved easily on its leather hinges when I lifted it slightly and pushed. I opened it only enough to give me entrance. But I didn't rush anything. I stood outside and listened carefully. The snoring continued. On the ground I saw a long chunk of firewood and picked it up. Flattening myself against the doorjamb, I slid through the open door and raised the club, ready to strike against anything that moved. Nothing did.

Slowly I lowered the club, though I kept a tight grip

on it. I looked around the tiny one-room *casa* a full minute, getting my bearings. I could see two people sleeping
on a cowhide bed, a slightly-built man and a rather stout
woman. They had a couple of blankets wrapped around
themselves. How I wanted one of those blankets! But any
kind of clothes would be an improvement. I saw the Mexican's shirt and trousers and a ragged old coat hanging
from a peg. Carefully I reached for them, took what I
thought was a firm hold and lifted. Something fell. It hit
the floor with a light thump. Instinctively I reached down
and grabbed. It was a knife in a leather scabbard.

The sound stirred the man. He raised up, blinking un-
easily. *"Qué es? Qué es?"* His movement awakened the
woman. She opened her eyes and saw me. She screamed.

The Mexican jumped out of bed and rushed me. I had
no choice but to use that chunk of firewood. It flattened
him.

The woman screamed again, her hands against her
cheeks. *"Americano!"* Before I could move, she had yanked
the door open and was running out into the night crying.
"Americano! Americano!"

On the floor the man swayed to his hands and knees.
I looked around desperately for a gun, any kind of gun.
There wasn't any. The man was pushing himself to his
feet. Out in the darkness the woman was running,
screaming. In a minute or two the neighbors would be
on their way. They wouldn't be friendly.

I wanted to ransack the house for food, but there
wasn't time now. I clutched their clothes under my arm,
determined to get away with at least that much, and hurried out the door. I stumbled over the rooster's crate and
sprawled on the ground.

By George, *there* was food. I gathered the stolen clothes
under my left arm and yanked the rooster out of his crate
with the right. Then I took off in a hard run. I didn't

stop running until my lungs arched and my legs seemed ready to buckle. Then I stopped and fell to the ground to rest. The rooster struggled. My first inclination was to eat him raw, for I was hungry enough. I knew I had to kill him right away, or he would more than likely get loose from me. I wrung his neck and waited for him to quit flopping. At least he had died for a better cause than someone's sport.

I put the Mexican's clothes on over my own. They fitted me better than I had any right to expect. And inside the pocket of the trousers I found a flint and steel.

My situation was still bad, but it was improving.

After gutting the rooster and resting for a little, I set out walking, moving in what I judged to be a northeasterly direction. I carried the dead rooster under my arm, for I couldn't afford to build a fire and cook him until daylight came to mask the flames.

When it was light I picked a good thicket and went into the heart of it. Using the flint and steel, and strips of cloth, I eventually got a small fire underway. The rooster was much too thin and stringy to be good eating, but this was no time or place to be choosy. Little as he was, he would be the best meal I had had in a long time. I impaled him on a spit, scorched him a little and ate him.

Exhausted, I slept most of the day. Terrible dreams of that awful massacre finally brought me wide awake, trembling. I lay there awhile, my eyes wide open. I had a horrible feeling that if I turned over and looked behind me I would find the Mexicans there with their muskets and lances, waiting to kill me. I managed after a bit to roll over. There was no one. I was alone.

My heart pounded from the terror of the dreams. My eyes burned with tears as the awful memories rushed back unbidden like floodwaters breaking through a dam.

My arms were swollen and sore, but that wouldn't slow my walking. Though still hungry, I had at least had a good rest. With the dark to shield me, I would set out walking. I could walk a long way before morning came again.

Chapter Sixteen

It was well that I had obtained the coat, for a norther blew in, bringing a cold, drizzling rain. With the bite of cold, hunger came back stronger than ever. That rooster had only whetted my appetite. It was a bad time of the year to find berries, wild fruit or pecans, for the first were out of season and the others had fallen to the ground to be picked up by the wild hogs, deer and other animals.

That was the ironic thing. All around me flocked an abundance of game—deer, wild turkeys. But without a gun I was unable to bring any of them to hand. The best I could find was some wild onions.

The third night my luck took a brief turn. I came across a tree where some of the turkeys roosted and managed to get one.

Not having seen a Mexican all day, I decided to risk building a fire to cook the turkey. Rain had left the wood wet. It took half the night to cut wet bark away from enough dead timber to have dry wood to burn. I got the turkey partially cooked, then ate it all except the feathers and bones. But much of my safe walking time had been wasted. And there was no telling how far I was from home. There hadn't been any familiar landmarks.

Hunger appeased, I decided to do some daylight traveling. The arm was still stiff but no longer painful except when I put pressure on it. With the new strength that came from a good meal, I was able to put some miles behind me. Instead of looking for a motte of timber when daylight came, I kept on walking.

In due time I came to a river and judged it to be the Guadalupe. It was running high and muddy from the heavy rains. My heart sagged. With this stiff arm, I probably could not swim it.

I gritted my teeth in disappointment. It would be a grim joke if I had escaped the firing squad at Goliad, only to drown here unseen, a hundred miles from home.

Upriver somewhere would be Gonzales, but it would do me no good to go there. Undoubtedly the Mexicans had it by now.

Somehow I had to find a way across that river but I had not the faintest notion what to do. I thought of trying to make a raft of some kind but had never done it before and didn't know just how to go about it. Besides, that current probably would be more than I could handle. It would likely carry me downriver a way and then dump me to drown.

Well, maybe something would turn up. I started walking upriver.

I had walked a long time when I heard the sound of moving horses. Mexicans, I figured. I flattened myself in undergrowth near the riverbank and strained to see.

When the horses came in sight, a chill ran down my back. It wasn't Mexicans, it was *Indians*.

Somehow, in my anxiety, I had considered only the danger of Mexicans. Now I realized I had an equally dangerous foe to watch for, because these appeared to be Comanches. Nothing would please a Comanche more than to come across a straggling Texian and lift his hair. I lay flat until they were well past me, moving downriver. Then I arose and left in a hurry.

In one way the Indians were even a greater threat than the Mexicans. They saw more. They were hunters born and bred. Their eyes could read meaning into a boottrack or a broken limb that might be overlooked by a Mexican or a Texian.

I came at length to a log cabin, or rather, the ruins of one. Only a blackened hull remained, with the charred roof caved in. Cautiously, crouching and taking my time, I picked my way through it, alert for sign of life. There was no evidence of battle. The owners probably had fled ahead of the enemy advance. More than likely Mexican soldiers had burned the cabin, or Indians had come along and done it. If there had been anything of value inside— clothes, for instance—it was gone now. I hoped to find something to eat—chickens or a hog or a milk cow's calf—that had been left behind. If there had been such, someone had beaten me to it. For me, the cabin was a total loss.

No, not quite. At the river bank, partially hidden by undergrowth, a small boat lay mostly submerged in the water. A short length of rawhide rope held it to a tree.

My one bad arm made it heavy pulling against the current. A determined effort finally brought the boat up out of the river. I turned it over to empty the water out and examined it carefully for sign of a hole. A few minutes' search produced the oars.

Now, at least, I was able to cross the river. On the far side I hid the boat and struck out walking again.

During the day I saw four Mexican horsemen. I was crossing an open prairie where last year's dry grass still stood tall and coarse. Dropping down in it, I lay unseen while they passed two hundred yards away. Later I saw a small band of Indians, though they were at a greater distance and were more of a scare than a threat.

I considered going back to my original plan—traveling at night and hiding by day. It was safer. But I was still a long way from home. I found myself worrying more and more about Muley, waiting there for me. With that boy's mind of his, he was probably frightened half to death. He might stay instead of running as I had told him to. He couldn't defend himself when the Mexicans came— if they had not already come. Because of Muley I decided to take my chances and keep traveling during at least part of the day.

My worst scare came the second day past the Guadalupe. Moving across the prairie, I spied a small cloud of dust. It was coming my way. Presently I heard hoofs. A troop of Mexican cavalry, or a band of Indians, I was certain. I tried to flatten and hide myself in the grass, but it was too short. It wouldn't hide me unless they were all blind. And they wouldn't be. The hoofbeats came closer.

I had my chin on the ground, but gradually I gathered my courage and raised my head to look. It was horses, all right, and they were coming upon me fast. But there wasn't a rider on them. They were wild mustangs, running free. I waited until I was sure no one was chasing them.

Then, afraid they might run over me, I stood up and waved my arms, shouting. The horses slid to a stop. They stood a moment watching me, their ears all cocked forward. They probably had never seen a man afoot. But they didn't care for what they saw. They wheeled around and galloped off, getting well in the clear. Then they stopped and turned to watch me some more, from a safer distance.

That night, just at dusk, I came upon the Mexican camp.

I would have done like the mustangs and gone way around, had I known. But I almost stumbled onto the camp before I saw it. They were cavalry, nearly twenty men. They had their horses tied on two picket lines, feeding them corn which they probably had found at some abandoned settler cabin. The soldiers were building up a campfire and preparing to cook supper.

I lay on my stomach and watched them. The wise thing, I knew, would be to ease myself well around them in the darkness and be long gone before morning. But the horses had caught my eye.

I had been walking for days. I knew I wasn't far from home now, but it might take me several more days to get there at the rate I was moving. With a horse, I could reduce the time.

The temptation was almost overwhelming. With my knife I could run in there, cut a horse loose and be gone before the single Mexican guard would have time to life his rifle. But it would be like punching at a hornet's nest with a stick. They would be after me in minutes. Whether I could get away or not would simply depend upon whether my luck was better than theirs.

I had seen enough of Mexican luck lately not to want to take the risk.

But I wouldn't leave until I had made a try of some kind. I lay and watched the soldiers cook and eat. My stomach growled. I had eaten only at irregular intervals, and the last interval had been a long one. I watched the dirty-uniformed men move about, and my mind inevitably turned back to that awful morning on the road to Copano. There was no way for me to know whether these men had personally had a hand in it. But they wore the same uniform, and that was enough. Hatred stirred in me. I thought of a dozen ways to kill them all, like finding their gunpowder and throwing it into the fire. But they were all crazy notions, too wild to work.

At length, their hunger satisfied, the Mexicans began wrapping themselves in their blankets and stretching out. They left one guard with the horses. The men quickly dropped off to sleep. From that, I guessed they had had a long, hard day. And so, probably, had the guard.

I crawled closer to the lone Mexican awake, who sat with his back to a live oak tree, his musket across his lap. The dry leaves rustled under me. The Mexican looked around, startled. I froze. For a moment it appeared he might get up and investigate, and I tensed, ready to run. But when he heard nothing more, he gradually relaxed. He probably thought it was some night-prowling animal.

The campfire burned low. Out in the darkness wolves began to howl. They had howled every night since I had escaped from Goliad. Once they had come so close that I had finally climbed a tree. The wolves made the horses restless. The Mexican spoke softly to them but didn't get up. After a long while I saw his head begin to tilt forward. It jerked as he came awake, then sagged again. He was too tired to hold out. I knew I had only to wait.

The longer I watched him, the more I thought about the Mexican officer who had come to us on Palm Sunday morning with the report that we were leaving for Copano. He had known what was about to happen, but he had lied to us with a smile on his lips. I fancied I could see a resemblance between this guard and that officer. I found my hand straying down to the handle of the knife. It would be easy to rise up and steal over to him and slit his throat. Hell, he deserved it. They *all* deserved it, I thought. I ground my teeth, struggling against the temptation.

Even dying, he might cry out and arouse the camp.

No, it was more important to get myself a horse. Vengeance could wait.

It seemed an hour before I heard his gentle snoring. His head was tilted forward onto his arms, his arms across his knees. I arose quietly and moved toward the picket line, the knife in my hand. For a long time I had studied the horses, making my choice.

I wanted very badly to cut all the horses loose and run them off. But I knew I could get shot doing it. I might get away with one horse, but not all of them.

The knife was dull. I had to saw on the rawhide. The horses stirred restlessly. I kept glancing back at the Mexican, thinking he would wake up at any moment. The leather finally parted. Carefully I backed my horse out of his place on the line. I led him in a slow walk, pausing only to pick up a bridle, blanket and saddle which lay there handy to my reach. I held onto them—and onto my breath—until I had the horse well away from the camp. Then I paused long enough to bridle and saddle him, swung up and was on my way.

The camp never stirred.

Chapter Seventeen

Once I struck the Colorado River, I had no trouble finding our place. I passed many others first. Without exception, they had been burned. My hopes sagged. The Mexicans had been here. No telling what had happened to Muley.

Though I nursed some faint hopes, I knew pretty well what to expect when I rode across the field. The winter wheat was growing fine. The corn had been planted—Muley's work. I slanted down the trail to our cabin. The cabin was gone, all but its blackened skeleton. I swallowed, anger rising momentarily. I eased the horse toward the cold ruins, looking for signs of Muley. Actually, though I wouldn't have admitted it, I was watching for his body.

I found no trace of him. When I felt safe in doing so, I began to call: "Muley! Muley! It's me, Josh!"

I had some thought that he might have hidden in the

timber. It would be like him. He might be there yet, waiting for somebody to come and get him. Waiting for me.

There wasn't a sign of Muley. But on a closer examination I found familiar dog tracks.

"Hickory!" I whistled a few times, then called again. "Here, Hickory!"

The old spotted hound slunk out of the timber, tail between his legs. He crouched uncertainly, knowing my voice but still not trusting.

I called him again and rode slowly toward him. Recognition came finally, and he fell to barking joyously, running at me, his tail wagging so hard he almost fell over. Always a chaser but never a hunter, he was thin and hungry-looking. That settled it: Muley was either dead or gone. He wouldn't have let the dog do without.

Hickory jumped all over me in his joy. He whimpered and cried while I petted him and tried to get him quieted down.

Now the worry I had carried for days turned to genuine fear. I knew from bitter experience what Santa Ana's soldiers were doing to prisoners. They might not have killed Muley here. They might have taken him to be killed somewhere else, on somebody's cruel whim.

Still, there was a chance Muley was all right. He might have run like I told him. From appearances, all the American settlers in this part of the country had pulled out hastily. Lots of people around here knew about Muley. Maybe somebody had taken enough time to come by and get him.

There was one place I might be able to find out. I found my eyes lifting to the trail I used to ride toward the Hernandez *rancho*. I couldn't be sure, of course, that the family was still there. They might have pulled out too. But I had noticed that by and large the Mexican families were tending to stay put as the American families fled. They didn't seem to feel they had much to fear from the Mexican soldiers. After all, they were of the same blood. A goodly percentage of them, as I had found to my sorrow, sided with the soldiers against us.

I couldn't know what reception to expect at the Hernandez place. I'd thought many times of the way Ramón Hernandez had hedged on an answer when I asked him which way he would go if it came to war. I'd remembered often the look in his eyes when I took him the news that his younger brother had been killed in the battle of San Antonio de Bexar.

Ramón might have gone over to Santa Ana's side by now. Friendship is one thing, but blood is another.

I sat on the hill a long while and surveyed the stone house before I touched my heels to the horse's ribs and started him down in an easy walk. Muley's hound tagged along close. He was sticking to me like a mesquite thorn.

The kids—Ramón's youngest brothers and sisters— played outside. A couple of horses stood droop-headed in a corral. Grazing cattle were scattered in the grassy draw and across the field.

The youngsters raised a frightened shout when they saw me. My beard had grown untouched for weeks and now was ragged and tangled and black. My clothes hung on me like they would on a scarecrow. I must have looked like some devilish apparition. There was, in those days, a strong tendency toward superstition in the Mexican people. Whatever or whoever they thought I was, they ran screaming into the house. The door slammed behind them. I heard the bar drop.

In a moment a shuttered window swung open. The barrel of an old musket poked out. A woman's voice cried, *Ándele! Ándele!* It was a way of saying to move along.

I raised my hands. In Spanish I called. "I am Josh Buckalew."

The musket was pulled back out of sight. The door opened cautiously. A young woman stood there, the musket still in her hands but no longer pointed directly at me.

"Josh, is it you? Is it really you?"

Weak, desperately hungry, I almost fell as I slid off the horse. I caught hold of the stirrup and pulled myself up. "Yes, María, it's me."

Hesitant, she came out under the brush arbor. Finally certain, she ran and threw her arms around me, musket and all.

"Josh, Josh, we thought you were dead!"

She hurt my arm, and I flinched. It never had healed completely. She stepped back, eyes wide in concern. "You are wounded."

"Not bad, still just a little raw. It'll be all right."

She hugged me again but went easy on the left arm. Then she studied my face. "You look terrible. Where have you been?" She didn't give me a chance to answer. "You shouldn't be here, Josh. Patrols come by every day or two. If they find you, they will kill you."

"I had to come. I need to talk to Ramón."

She shook her head. "Ramón has gone to the army."

My breath stopped for a moment. "The Mexican army?"

"No, Sam Houston's army. He went to fight Santa Ana."

The relief that came to me was only momentary. "María, I can't find Muley. I hoped Ramón could tell me what happened to him."

"Muley is all right, or was. Ramón was afraid to leave him by himself with Santa Ana's army on the way. He made Muley go with him to join Sam Houston."

I sighed. A terrible weight slipped from my shoulders. "Thanks to God, María." For a minute all I could think about was that Muley was all right. Then I glanced toward the door and saw Ramón's wife. Miranda stared, still not sure who I was.

"María." I demanded, "why did Ramón leave the rest of you here? Why didn't he take you and run?"

"It was too near Miranda's time. She could not travel. We decided we would be safe here. We are Mexicans. We thought the soldiers would not hurt us. And it has been true. Many have been here, but none have done us any harm.

I frowned, remembering the trouble Miranda had had with her first baby. "You will need help with her, María."

"When Ramón left, it was all arranged. Señora Ramirez is a midwife, and she was going to stay. But her husband became frightened and took her east with the rest of the runaways. So I will have to do the job myself."

"Can you?"

"I have been told what to do. I will do the best I can." She took my good arm. "Come, Miranda and the children are frightened. They still don't know who you are."

Miranda hugged me and cried a little. The children cautiously shook my hand, but the smaller ones were still unconvinced that I was not some kind of devil. María set about cooking beef for me. I took a pair of scissors and clipped away most of my beard. I then borrowed an old razor that had belonged to María's father and shaved my face clean.

As I ate, I told them briefly what had happened to me. I skipped most of the details, for the thought of them still made my blood go cold. I trembled as I told how Thomas had been butchered. The women wept silently.

I intended to leave after I had eaten and ride through the night. But I was so weary I thought I would lie down on one of the cowhide cots and rest an hour or so. When I awoke, it was morning. I sat bolt upright, staring in confusion and alarm. The women were preparing breakfast.

"María," I demanded, "why did you let me sleep?"

"You needed the rest. See, you look better already."

"I've got to move on. I want to catch up with Houston's army."

"You will eat first."

Impatience was like needles prickling my skin, but she was right. I had needed the rest. And I needed another good meal, for it might be a long time before the next one. So I sat on the cot and watched the woman. Miranda moved slowly because of her size. María tried to get her to sit down, but she would not. I watched María particularly. It struck me that she had changed a lot since the first time I had seen her. She was a woman now, moving with purpose and sureness. And, she was a pretty woman.

I was eating when one of the boys ran into the house. "*Soldados!*" Soldiers were coming.

I jumped to my feet. "I'd better run. It'll go hard on you if they find me here."

Muley's dog was barking wildly. María glanced out the window. "Too late, they are too close. We'll have to hide you."

I thought of the horse and the Mexican saddle I had stolen. They would be a dead giveaway.

María shook her head. "I had Pepe turn the horse loose. We hid your saddle under the hay. Come!"

She let me out the back door. We glanced around for some place I could get out of sight. I saw nothing but the woodpile. I sprinted around that and dropped flat on my belly. I lay there with the knife in my hand, the only weapon I had. If found, I intended to sell out at a high price.

I heard the horses at the front of the house, and Hickory's barking. One of the soldiers must have hurled something at the dog, for he yelped in terror and ran around behind the house. He caught my scent and came crying to me.

"Get away, Hickory! Git!"

He wouldn't leave me. He tried to crowd in with me behind the woodpile. My mouth went dry, for I was afraid one of the soldiers might follow Hickory around the house to chunk at him again. None did.

"Damn you. Hickory, I ought to cut your cowardly throat."

But he stayed. It was a long time before I heard the patrol start moving away. Hickory ventured forth to bark at the soldiers from a respectful distance. Cautiously I peeked out to watch the horsemen moving eastward, singing. One of them paused to throw a rock back at Hickory.

I stayed put until finally María came.

"They are well gone," she said, as I got to my feet.

"They sure stayed a while."

"They made us cook for them."

"They didn't hurt you?"

"We told them our men had gone to help Santa Ana. They didn't hurt us."

"María, I've got to leave here. The longer I stay the more dangerous it is for you and for me."

She nodded gravely. "I'll have the boys bring you a fresh horse. We had to hide the good horses from the runaways. They took all they could find."

We returned to the house, María gave orders to the older boys, and they hit the door in a run. Turning to Miranda, I found her trembling. "Please, Josh," she said, "do not think I always am this foolish. It is my time and my condition, I suppose. I was frightened to death."

Taking her hand, I tried to give her reassurance. "I'll be gone in a few minutes. Then you won't have to worry."

A twinge of pain creased Miranda's olive face. "I think I have much to worry about. I think the time has come."

María's eyes widened. She glanced at me, then at Miranda. "You could be wrong, Miranda. Remember, there was that other alarm two days ago."

Miranda paled, flinching again. "This time, I think, it is real. The excitement has been too much." She cried out as a sharp pain hit her. It looked as if she would fall. I grabbed her.

"María, what do we do now?"

María's lips tightened. "I suppose we will deliver the baby."

The boys brought my horse up outside, saddled and ready to go. But there was no leaving now.

"María, I've never been around where a woman was having a baby."

"Then we shall both learn together."

Mostly I stood by and did whatever María said to do, while Miranda bit her lips and gripped the wooden edge of the bedframe, fighting against the pain.

The children were kept outside, watching for another patrol. María and I bustled about, making the preparations she thought were necessary. When the time came for delivery. I turned my face away and left that part up to María. I held Miranda's hands. Or rather, she held mine, digging her fingernails in, gritting her teeth to keep from crying out.

"Cry if you want to, Miranda," I said. "Sometimes it's better."

But she shook her head. She had no intention of giving in to the pain.

Then, suddenly, the baby was there. María clutched it in her hands, a tiny reddish-brown thing.

"Josh," she cried, "Josh, do something! It's not breathing. Josh!"

The breath had not started. I saw the fear in Miranda's eyes, and in María's. I remembered something I had heard about spanking a new baby's bottom. I took the infant in my left hand and tapped its backside smartly with the palm of my right.

I felt a quiver of life, then heard the whimper that lifted into a cry. I looked at María. Relief flooded her face. She smiled, then laughed thinly. Her laugh grew louder, and I was laughing with her, the baby still dangling from my hand. María threw her arms around me. We stood there holding each other and laughed like a pair of fools.

Later I watched María tuck the blanket around Miranda and the baby. "María," I said, "you're a wonder."

I found myself studying her again as I had at breakfast, admiring the quick and easy way she moved, the slimness of her, the pleasant eyes and face. She was conscious of the way I appraised her, for color rose in her cheeks.

I said, "It's amazing to me, the way you resemble Teresa."

"I am not Teresa," she said pointedly. "I am María. I shall always be María. I would never be a substitute for someone else."

"I didn't mean it that way," I said hastily, realizing I had hurt her. "I would always want you to be yourself. I would always want you to be the way you have been today. With all respect to Teresa. I doubt she would ever have been able to do what you've done."

María said, "Teresa was my sister, and I shall always love her memory. But she was weak, Josh. Had *I* loved a man, I would have turned my back on family and all. I would have spit in the devil's eye to have him. I would never have married someone else because it was expected of me and I had not the courage to say no."

"No," I said with admiration, "I don't suppose you would."

The children came in to look at the new baby. One of the smaller ones marveled that he hadn't seen anybody come and bring it. Smiling wisely, an older boy said, "Your horse is here, Josh, and we see no soldiers."

"Thanks, *muchacho*. I guess I'd better leave."

Miranda called me to her bedside. "Josh, if you see Ramón, tell him I will be waiting for him. Tell him I have given him another son."

I squeezed her hand. "I'll tell him. He'll be proud of you."

María walked out with me, carrying a sack of food she had prepared. She also had the old musket.

"We do not need the gun, Josh. You might."

I took her arm and pulled her up close. I didn't want to leave. "María, if this war ends in our favor, I'll be back. I'd like to come and visit you, if you'll let me."

Her eyes glistened. "Will you be coming to see me, or will you really be seeing Teresa?' "

"Teresa was a long time ago. That is over. I'll be coming to see you, María."

"Then come back, Josh. Come back soon."

She clutched my arm and leaned forward and kissed me.

I swung into the saddle and rode away, looking back over my shoulder.

Chapter Eighteen

This was a time that would ever after be known in Texas as the "runaway escape." American settlers packed what possessions they could carry and left the rest behind them as they fled in their wagons or on horseback or afoot—often in panic—before the onslaught of Mexican troops. The news of the Alamo and Goliad had put an icy chill in Texian veins. A cold, hard fury set in, and a desperate desire for revenge. But there were practical matters to be attended to. Family men left Sam Houston's ranks to hurry home and see that their loved ones were evacuated to the sanctuary that waited for them across the Sabine.

It was a cold, rainy time, with mud that mired wagons to the hubs. Open prairies became vast lakes that sometimes had to be forded. Indians and Mexican guerrillas harassed the stragglers, striking and lashing and running away. Sickness swept the struggling caravans of wagons and carts and sleds.

How many died and were left behind in this awful backwash of war, no one ever really knew. The toll was heavy among women and children.

And all this time Sam Houston's dwindling army retreated, seething for revenge, falling back to first one river, then another—avoiding any full-scale clash. Houston was buying time, giving the runaways an opportunity to reach safety, waiting for the chance to strike the Mexicans when the odds were in the Texians' favor. Always outnumbered, always held back by Houston's caution, the Texians wondered if they would ever get that chance. Impatience turned to anger, and slowly anger built toward open mutiny.

But, grim as the crowded bear, Houston stood up to the abuse and the criticism. His was the only fighting force Texas had left. Texas could not stand another defeat. When he committed his men to battle, he wanted to know they had a better than even chance of winning. If they lost, the war was over, and Texas was gone.

I finally caught up to Houston's army opposite Harrisburg. That had been the capital of the newly-declared Republic of Texas, though by now the officials of the government had fled. Santa Ana had already been to Harrisburg and had left it in ashes.

I had come across many Mexican patrols and details of cavalry since leaving the Colorado River. I always kept out of their sight. I had trailed the retreating army to Groce's plantation. East of the McCurley place I came to the fork in the road. The left-hand fork was the trace leading toward the Sabine and safety. The right-hand fork led toward Harrisburg, and a certain head-on clash with Santa Ana. Though it had rained heavily, and two or three days had passed, I could still tell where the army had gone. It had taken the right-hand fork.

I had a feeling I was getting close now. I hadn't seen a Mexican in some time. Sitting in a clump of timber, I watched four horsemen coming my way, rifles across their laps. I took them to be Texians, though I hid myself until they were close enough that I knew for sure. Then I rode out into the open.

They hauled up quickly, their rifles swinging toward me. I raised my right hand and moved on, slower now.

"All right, friend," one of them said, staring at me over the barrel of his rifle, "before you come any closer we want to know who you are."

"I'm a Texian, I was at Goliad."

The man lowered his rifle. I got a look at his face, and a chill touched me. I knew him from somewhere, and it wasn't a pleasant memory. I reached back in my mind to long ago. Natchitoches. That was the face I had seen at Natchitoches so many long years ago. Lige, his name had been.

I knew a bitter moment then. Had I escaped from Goliad, dodged Mexicans and Indians across most of Texas, only to fall into the hands of cutthroats?

Lige squinted. "By George, I do believe I know you from someplace. Where have I seen you at?"

I said, "Try Natchitoches, several years back. You and some friends of yours tried to rob us on the trail to the Sabine."

Recognition came, and with it a moment of astonishment. Then, a broad grin. "Well, if that don't beat all. That was a long time, boy, for the chickens to finally come to roost. Been a lot of changes made."

"I doubt if you've changed much," I said.

He still grinned. "I know what you're thinkin', but I long since give up my sinful ways. You boys kind of give me a push in that direction. We're fightin' on the same side now, boy. A lot of us have had to turn our backs on old feuds and face the Mexicans together. Goliad, you say? And you got away? Rememberin' Natchitoches, I can't say as I'm surprised none. Come on, we'll take you to camp."

My arrival caused a stir, though I found out I wasn't the first Goliad survivor to catch up with the army. Several had made it here before me, individually picking their way across Texas just as I had done.

I was taken directly to Sam Houston's tent. He sat there and stared at me, a huge man with a strong, square face and piercing eyes. He reached into the pocket of his black coat and took out a bottle of salts of hartshorn, which he applied to his nostrils as I told him briefly what had happened to me.

"You've been through hell enough," he said finally. "You should have gone on to the Sabine instead of coming here."

I shook my head. "Not many of us got away from Goliad, General. I figure I owe a debt to all those who didn't."

Houston's jaw ridged. He glanced at his officers. "Has this man been fed?" When they said I hadn't, he ordered, "Then take him and feed him. See if you can find him a decent rifle and something to put in it."

I saluted him and turned to go. Houston called after me, "You can still go across the Sabine if you've a mind to. You've done your share."

"If it's all the same to you, General, I'll stay." In fact, I had made up my mind to stay whether it was all right with him or not.

One of the officers led me to a small company which he commanded. "Here's a man from Goliad. Feed him."

I wolfed the food down. As I was finishing up I said,

"Major, I'm lookin' for a friend of mine, a partner. Name is Muley Dodd."

He shook his head. "We have almost eight hundred men in this camp. I couldn't know them all."

"He's supposed to have come with a Mexican friend of mine named Ramón Hernandez. You'd probably remember Muley if you came across him. He's . . . a little slow. He's not real bright."

One of the men said, "Major, I'll bet I know who he's huntin'. There was a little feller came into camp with a Mexican while we was at Groce's. The Mexican joined up with Juan Seguin's company. The little feller stayed with him. A bunch of us tried to talk him into joinin' a white man's outfit, but he wouldn't. Stuck to that Mexican like a pet dog."

I said, "That'd be Muley. Take me to him."

The name Seguin was familiar. The Seguins were a wealthy Mexican family, with large landholdings around San Antonio. General Cos had mistreated old Erasmo Seguin. As a result the Seguin family sided with the Texians with their land, their cattle, their money and their arms. Juan Seguin, I was told, had been in the Alamo in the early part of the siege, but Travis had sent him out as a courier. There had been no returning.

The officer led me across the camp to where the Seguin company had bivouacked. A shudder ran through me as I looked at the dark faces and listened to the rapid flow of soft-spoken Spanish. Though these men were on our side, and though a few months ago I would have found it easy to call any of them friend, bitter memories stood between us now. I found myself blaming them all for being Mexicans.

"I am looking for Muley Dodd," I said in Spanish.

"The little *Americano?* He is here somewhere with Ramón Hernandez." He called. "*Señor* Dodd! *Dónde está?*"

I saw a slight figure rise up from some muddy blankets and look around wide-eyed. "Muley!" I broke into a run toward him. He jumped to his feet. "Josh! Josh! Josh!" he grabbed me, and we hugged each other. Muley began crying. "Josh, Ramón said you was likely dead. But I told him you wouldn't be. I told him you promised to come and get me, and you didn't never break any promise you ever made. I told him you wouldn't let them old Mexicans kill you if it was goin' to go ag'in your promise."

I clenched his shoulder and stood back to stare at him. He looked about the same as ever, except a little thinner. Rations hadn't come regularly.

Another voice broke in. "Josh, it is good to see you."

I turned to Ramón Hernandez and gave him the *abrazo*. He smiled broadly. "I thought Santa Ana had nailed you up with his trophies."

I said, "He did get Thomas."

Ramón's smile disappeared. He gripped my arm in sympathy. "Now we have each lost a brother. Where did it happen?"

Once again I told it. The Mexicans gathered and listened, those who could understand English.

Ramón said, "And so now you want to fight, to get even."

"It's somethin' I've got to do."

"This is a good company, Juan Seguin's. We would like you to join us."

I looked around me at the dark faces, the black eyes. Again I felt that uncomfortable stirring. I knew it was unfair, but I couldn't help it. Friends or not, when I looked at them I would see those other dark faces at Goliad, peering at us down the barrels of their rifles.

"Thanks, Ramón. But after what I've been through . . ." I tried to find the words to explain and couldn't. "It's nothin' personal, it's just . . . Well, I'd best find a place among my own people. I'll take Muley with me."

Ramón was silent a moment, perhaps hurt a little, though he didn't show it. "In your situation, I would be the same. It took me a long time to decide that my place was here."

I started to go, then turned back. "Ramón, I went by the *rancho*. You have another son."

"She is all right, my Miranda?"

"She came through fine. Said tell you to hurry home."

"We shall soon see if *any* of us go home."

We were waiting to cross Buffalo Bayou when Houston rode into the center of the army on his big white stallion Saracen. Far in the distance we could see smoke. Santa Ana was burning everything as he moved.

Houston sat on that big stud and made us a speech. He said we would win the battle that lay ahead, that we would have vengeance for those who had fallen in the Alamo. For those slaughtered at Goliad.

"Remember the Alamo!" he thundered. "Remember Goliad!"

It became a war cry. It spread through the army like a brushfire. Men raised their rifles over their heads and shouted the words over and over again. "Remember the Alamo! Remember Goliad!"

San Jacinto. Moving down Buffalo Bayou, we reached the San Jacinto River on April 20. Houston ordered us into camp in a grove of live oaks. Buffalo Bayou to our backs, the San Jacinto to our left. In front of us lay a pretty stretch of open prairie, rising slightly toward groves of moss-strewn live oak trees.

Later in the afternoon the cry went up. "The Mexicans are coming!"

We already knew that, for scouts had been bringing in reports at regular intervals. They said this was Santa Ana himself. We prepared ourselves for attack. With the river and the bayou at our flank and our back, and with Santa Ana coming up in front of us, we were in no position anymore to retreat. If the Mexicans came, we had to stand our ground and fight.

They didn't come. Santa Ana went into camp on the opposite side of the prairie, a broad lake to one side of him, the marshes behind him. He sounded us out by sending forward a six-pounder with a detachment of cavalry for protection. The cannon opened up. Some said Santa Ana probably hoped we would reply with musket fire and give him a good idea how we were lined up. On orders, we held our fire and answered him only with a few rounds from the Twin Sisters, a matched pair of cannon recently arrived as a gift from the people of Cincinnati.

There was one brief cavalry skirmish that afternoon as a group of volunteers attempted to rush forward and take the Mexican cannon. They failed to get the cannon but came back satisfied they had drawn blood.

The night was cold but quiet. Our scouts brought the report next morning that General Cos had arrived with reinforcements for Santa Ana. They had us outnumbered now by a little less than two to one.

This, then, was the time to fight, if we ever were going to fight. Some of the officers quarreled over it, but the men were of a temper to go ahead, with officers or without them. It was about three o'clock in the afternoon of April 21 that Houston ordered us paraded and announced that we were not going to wait for Santa Ana to come to us. We were going to go to *him*.

With the Twin Sisters in the center of the line, infantry

on both sides, and cavalry on the right flank, we stretched out for some nine hundred yards.

There was a popular song in those days, a simple little tune called "Come to the Bower." A love song, not a battle song. But now the drummer and three fifers struck it up.

Will you come to the bower I have shaded for you?
Our bed shall be roses all spangled with dew.
There under the bower of roses you lie
With a blush on your cheek but a smile in your eye.

Astride the big white stallion, Sam Houston rode all the way across the long line, making an inspection. What he found was a motley gathering of buckskins and home-spuns and clawhammer coats, of farmers and hunters, lawyers and locksmiths, preachers and teachers and sin-ners and saints. Done, he returned to the center of the line. He sat there a moment, looking back, then looking forward. He shouted a command that I couldn't hear. He dropped his arm. The ragged line began to move across that stretch of open prairie toward the camp of Santa Ana.

The cavalry rode far around on the left to create a diversion. The rest of us walked through the grass, our rifles ready. In the center, artillerymen pulled the Twin Sisters along on rawhide ropes.

The order was to hold our fire until we crested the hill and were well within range. We all walked silently, each of us going back over his own reasons for being here. I felt a prickling of my skin. My hands clutched the rifle I had been given to replace the old Hernandez musket. I knew fear, for I had learned at San Antonio and at Go-liad how terrible a battle can be. But I knew also a fresh sense of anger, for now once again I saw Thomas, and I saw all those tragic men with whom I had spent that miserable time in the fortress at Goliad. In my mind I heard again the rattle of musketry, heard the screams of the helpless dying men as they fell on the Copano road. I found myself walking faster and faster, the sound of remembered gunfire exploding in my ears. I found myself muttering quietly. "Goliad. Goliad. This is going to be for Goliad."

We topped over the rise. Now there came a scattering of riflefire from the Mexican camp. But we saw comparatively few Mexican soldiers. Most of their rifles were stacked.

Siesta! We had caught them at *siesta!*

A Mexican cannon boomed. Our own artillerymen stopped and fired the Twin Sisters. They reloaded and came again, pulling the two cannons closer.

Now that the firing had opened up, men began running. They were shouting, too.

"Remember the Alamo! Remember Goliad!"

The Mexicans of Seguin's company took up the cry in Spanish. *"Recuerden el Alamo!"* The shouts rose up like thunder.

On the far left, the cavalry tore into the Mexican line with a crushing fury.

The Mexican fire was still weak, but it was starting to count. Houston's white stallion went down. Almost instantly someone brought Houston another horse. He remounted, only to go down again, this time with a bullet in his own leg.

Shouting at the tops of our lungs, we raged into the Mexican line, firing, slashing with our bayonets, swinging our rifle butts. The Mexicans who had tried to return our fire went down in those first moments. The others, caught asleep, tried desperately to reach their stacked arms. Most of them never made it.

Riderless Mexican horses galloped through the camp, running over tents in their panic, trampling *soldados* who did not scramble out of their way in time.

Here and there soldiers stopped in their flight to turn and fire at us, but their aim was erratic. Most of the Mexicans simply ran, leaving their weapons behind them.

It has been said that the battle of San Jacinto went on for hours.

The fleeing Mexicans found themselves trapped by the bayou. Some dived in and tried to swim, many bogging down hopelessly in the mud. Others cowered at the bank, turning helplessly to face the Texian fire. And it was merciless fire, for these men were primed to fury by Santa Ana's vicious slaughter across the entire face of Texas. The screaming *soldados* raised their hands in supplication, only to be cut down.

I had been firing until my rifle barrel was so hot to the touch that it was hard to reload it. As I pushed to ram powder and ball for another shot, I saw a running Mexican confront a bayonet-wielding Texian. He dropped to his knees and cried out, "Me no Alamo! Me no Goliad!"

The Texian rammed the bayonet through the man's heart, put his foot against the body and jerked the rifle free.

It was no longer a battle. It was a hell of shouting, shooting, screaming men, of panic-stricken riderless horses dashing back and forth, of thundering cannon— our own now, altogether.

Through the smoke I saw a rider loping toward me. I could tell by the uniform that he was Mexican. I raised the rifle to draw a bead. He came through the smoke. I saw his face and gasped.

Antonio Hernandez!

I couldn't shoot. I lowered the rifle. He had his sword

raised to strike me, but he recognized me and hesitated.

Beside me, another Texian's rifle roared. The bullet took Antonio in the chest. He jerked backward and toppled to the ground as the frightened horse surged forward, almost running me down.

I turned to see who had fired. It was the one-time highwayman Lige. "I swear, boy, you was about to let that Meskin git away!"

I dropped to one knee beside Antonio. The life was ebbing out of him.

I don't know just what had happened to me then. A cold fury swept over me, a fury at this whole useless, senseless war, a fury for what had happened to Thomas, to all the men at Goliad.

In front of me stood a Mexican officer, no weapon left to him but a saber. I fired and missed. He charged at me, swinging the blade, I raised my rifle and let it take the force of the blow. The saber slid down the barrel, bounced off, caught my arm and ripped into my sleeve. I felt the deep bite of the steel. But I had too much momentum built to stop now. I swung the rifle butt around and caught him in the stomach. Much of the breath burst out of him.

But he managed to bring up the blade again. Once more I blocked it with the rifle, and this time I stepped in close and gave him a blow in the groin. He stiffened.

My imagination swept me away. For a second I looked at that face and thought I saw the officer who had spoken to us that morning at Goliad, the one who had smiled and led us like a Judas goat leads sheep to the slaughter.

The fury took over. I brought the rifle butt up and caught him under the chin. I pounded him in the face until he fell. In a black rage I used the rifle as a club to pound him and pound him and pound him, taking out on this man all the pent-up bitterness I had carried with me these long weeks.

Finally someone touched my shoulder. I whirled, the bloody rifle ready to strike again. It was Lige.

"Boy, he's as dead as he'll ever be."

That voice brought me crashing down to reality. I shook my head and blinked. Through the gray smoke I could see a vague swirling of figures. Texians still moving on in pursuit of fleeing soldiers. I could hear the ragged pattern of shooting, of continued slaughter. It would go on until darkness finally came to bring it to an end.

But for me, the battle was over. Santa Ana had been destroyed. The Alamo and Goliad had had their bloody vengeance.

It was over, and the fury I had brought with me was spent.

I raised my arm and found blood flowing slowly where the saber had taken its cut.

Lige said, "Boy, you better go and get somebody to see after that arm."

I nodded. I dropped the rifle and walked back in a daze, gripping the arm, the warm blood trickling out between my fingers. But I felt no pain. I felt only a vast relief. It was over now. It had to be.

I sat under a big live oak tree, wearily leaning back against its rough trunk while the doctor wrapped clean cloth around the cut to stop its bleeding. Across the way I could see Sam Houston lying on his blankets beneath another tree, his wounded leg stretched out in front of him. Whatever the pain he suffered—and it was great— he must have been feeling an intense satisfaction. This battle, this victory, was a vindication of his long weeks of silent retreat, of watchful waiting.

Slowly the various companies began to re-form. Weak from the shock of the wound, I nevertheless had to satisfy myself that Muley and Ramón had come through all right. I had told Muley to stay behind.

I found Muley alive, whole and jubilant. "Josh," he announced proudly, "I fought in that battle. They gave me a rifle and I used it and fought and didn't even run. You ought to be proud of me, Josh. I didn't run this time."

I gripped his shoulder. "I *am* proud of you, Muley."

Muley went with me as I hunted for Juan Seguin's company. It was still badly scattered, but after a long search I found Ramón. His face was begrimed, sweat still running down and leaving tiny trails of mud. He was exhausted, but he didn't show a scratch. He looked at me in alarm, but I assured him it was no worse than I had already received once before, at Goliad.

"It's been a hard day, Josh," he said. "But it was a great victory."

I nodded soberly. "A great victory." I tried to find a soft way to tell him, but there wasn't any.

"Ramón. I saw Antonio."

He read the rest of it in my eyes. "Dead?" I nodded. His eyes closed a moment, and his mouth went hard. Then: "He chose his own way. But he was my brother. Do you think you could find him for me?"

"I could try."

We picked our way across that red-soaked battlefield. Mexican soldiers lay all around us, crumpled in a hundred different attitudes of death. Now that the smoke was lifted and most of the noise and excitement were gone, it was a sickening sight. Muley's face was pale, but he found the courage to stick close beside me, and not turn back.

"There he is, Ramón," I said, pointing.

Ramón dropped to his knees beside his brother's body. He lifted the still hand and felt for a pulse. Gently he eased the hand down, removed his hat and made the sign of the cross. He knelt there a long time, while we stood in patient silence.

"He is of the enemy," Ramón said finally. "But I will ask General Houston to let me take him home and bury him among our own."

They brought in Santa Ana next day. A great hue and cry arose in camp to hang him, but Houston said no. He argued that Santa Ana, for all his bloody deeds, was of more use to Texas alive than dead. Dead men sign no treaties.

Up to the time of the battle, I would have shouted as loudly as anyone else for Santa Ana's death. But somehow San Jacinto had taken the bitterness out of me. Clubbing the life out of that officer had drained me of anger.

Ramón came to me and said, "Josh, I have permission to leave for home, and to take Antonio."

I could tell it was a way of asking me to go without bringing the question straight out.

"Josh," he continued, "I know you have had some bitter times, and you have had terrible things done to you by Mexican people. But I still consider you my friend."

He turned away, leading a packhorse with its sad burden tied securely.

I glanced at Muley. "When did you plant the corn?"

"First of March, just like you told me to."

"It ought to need plowin' about now, wouldn't you think?"

Muley nodded. "I expect it needs it pretty bad."

I called. "Ramón, hold up. Wait, and we'll all go home together."

Kelton on Kelton

I was born at a place called Horse Camp on the Scharbauer Cattle Company's Five Wells Ranch in Andrews County, Texas, in 1926. My father was a cowboy there, and my grandfather was the ranch foreman. My great-grandfather had come out from East Texas about 1876 with a wagon and a string of horses to become a ranchman, but he died young, leaving four small boys to grow up as cowpunchers and bronc breakers. With all that heritage I should have become a good cowboy myself, but somehow I never did, so I decided if I could not do it I would write about it.

I studied journalism at the University of Texas and became a livestock and farm reporter in San Angelo, Texas, writing fiction as a sideline to newspaper work. I have maintained the two careers in parallel more than thirty years. My fiction has been mostly about Texas, about areas whose history and people I know from long study and long personal acquaintance. I have always believed we can learn much about ourselves by studying our history, for we are the products of all that has gone before us. All history is relevant today, because the way we live—the values we believe in—are a result of molds prepared for us by our forebears a long time ago.

I was an infantryman in World War II and married an Austrian girl, Anna, I met there shortly after the war. We raised three children, all grown now and independent, proud of their mixed heritage of the Old World on one hand and the Texas frontier on the other.

PUBLISHER'S NOTE

Elmer Kelton was named the Greatest Western Writer of All Time by the Western Writers of America in 1995.

Westerns available from

TRAPPER'S MOON • Jory Sherman

"Jory Sherman takes us on an exhilarating journey of discovery with a colorful group of trappers and Indians. It is quite a ride."—Elmer Kelton

CASHBOX • Richard S. Wheeler

"A vivid portrait of the life and death of a frontier town."—*Kirkus Reviews*

SHORTGRASS SONG • Mike Blakely

"*Shortgrass Song* leaves me a bit stunned by its epic scope and the power of the writing. Excellent!"—Elmer Kelton

CITY OF WIDOWS • Loren Estleman

"Prose as picturesque as the painted desert…"—*The New York Times*

BIG HORN LEGACY • W. Michael Gear

Abriel Catton receives the last will and testament of his father, Web, and must reassemble his family to search for his father's legacy, all the while pursued by the murdering Braxton Bragg and desire for revenge and gold.

SAVAGE WHISPER • Earl Murray

When Austin Well's raid is foiled by beautiful Indian warrior Eagle's Shadow Woman, he cannot forget the beauty and ferocity of the woman who almost killed him or figure out a way to see her again.

Available by mail from

1812 • David Nevin
The War of 1812 would either make America a global power sweeping to the pacific or break it into small pieces bound to mighty England. Only the courage of James Madison, Andrew Jackson, and their wives could determine the nation's fate.

PRIDE OF LIONS • Morgan Llywelyn
Pride of Lions, the sequel to the immensely popular *Lion of Ireland,* is a stunningly realistic novel of the dreams and bloodshed, passion and treachery, of eleventh-century Ireland and its lusty people.

WALTZING IN RAGTIME • Eileen Charbonneau
The daughter of a lumber baron is struggling to make it as a journalist in turn-of-the-century San Francisco when she meets ranger Matthew Hart, whose passion for nature challenges her deepest held beliefs.

BUFFALO SOLDIERS • Tom Willard
Former slaves had proven they could fight valiantly for their freedom, but in the West they were to fight for the freedom and security of the white settlers who often despised them.

THIN MOON AND COLD MIST • Kathleen O'Neal Gear
Robin Heatherton, a spy for the Confederacy, flees with her son to the Colorado Territory, hoping to escape from Union Army Major Corley, obsessed with her ever since her espionage work led to the death of his brother.

SEMINOLE SONG • Vella Munn
"As the U.S. Army surrounds their reservation in the Florida Everglades, a Seminole warrior chief clings to the slave girl who once saved his life after fleeing from her master, a wifemurderer who is out for blood." —*Hot Picks*

THE OVERLAND TRAIL • Wendi Lee
Based on the authentic diaries of the women who crossed the country in the late 1840s. America, a widowed pioneer, and Dancing Feather, a young Paiute, set out to recover America's kidnapped infant daughter—and to forge a bridge between their two worlds.

Tex - mex
war
alamo & goliad

7 - '96, & 8 - '02, 12-12, 11-16

good